BRENDA COSTIGAN

Easy Does It

COOKBOOK

Crescent Press

© **Brenda Costigan**

Printed November 1995

ISBN 0-9514115-2-7

Photography - Neil Macdougald

Cooking and Food Styling - Brenda Costigan

Colour separations by Pentacolour
Printed at Aston Colour Press Ltd.

Published by Cresent Press (Publishers)
3 Sycamore Crescent,
Mount Merrion,
Co. Dublin, Ireland.

A catalogue record for this book is available from the British Library.

My sincere thanks to David Mc Donald for his excellent typing and editing skills. Special thanks to Catherine Mc Donald for her advice. Thanks also to Sarah O'Donnell and Peter Mc Donald for their helpful editing skills.

My sincere thanks also to Neil Macdougald for his expert advice.

For Dick - who made it all possible - with love.

Conversion Tables

All these are approximate conversion, which have either been rounded up or down. Never mix metric and imperial measures in one recipe; stick to one system or the other.

Weights	
½ oz	10g-15g
1	25
1½	40
2	50
3	75
4	110
5	150
6	175
7	200
8	225
9	250
10	275
12	350
13	375
14	400
15	425
1 lb	450
1¼	550
1½	700
2	900
3	1·4 kg
4	1·8
5	2·3

Volume	
1 fl oz	25 ml
2	50
3	75
5 (¼ pint)	150
10 (½)	275
15 (¾)	425
1 pint	570
1¼	700
1½	900
1¾	1 litre
2	1·1
2¼	1·3
2½	1·4
2¾	1·6
3	1·75
3¼	1·8
3½	2
3¾	2·1
4	2·3
5	2·8
6	3·4
7	4·0
8 (1 gal)	4·5

Measurements	
¼ inch	0·5 cm
½	1
1	2·5
2	5
3	7·5
4	10
5	12·5
6	15
7	18
8	20·5
9	23
11	28
12	30·5

Oven temperatures		
Mark 1	275°F	140°C
2	300	150
3	325	170
4	350	180
5	375	190
6	400	200
7	425	220
8	450	230
8	475	240

American			Imperial		Metric
Liquid	1 pt = 16 fluid oz	=	1 pt = 20 fluid oz	=	570 ml
	1 cup	=	8 fluid oz	=	225 ml
Chocolate	1 square	=	1 oz	=	25 g
Flour	2 cups	=	1 lb	=	450 g
Sugar	2½ cups	=	1 lb	=	450 g
Butter	1 stick	=	4 oz	=	110 g

Contents

Introduction

Don't you agree, that one of the things that gives a cook great pleasure is to see family and friends enjoy the food that he/she has prepared. Another pleasure is to share favourite recipes. I hope you will enjoy my latest collection of favourite recipes. Many of them have a Mediterranean flavour, using lots of vegetables and including oil (preferably olive oil). I have covered a wide variety of dishes, some very quick and easy, some just a little special... others a little indulgent!

With all the thousands of meals we consume in a life time, isn't it wonderful to take pleasure in their preparation, as well as the enjoyment of eating them.

Happy Cooking,

Brenda Costigan

For the convenience of those who have my other two cookery books ANYTHING I CAN DO, and FOR GOODNESS SAKE, I include the list of recipes from each of them at the back of this cookbook.

This will make it much easier and quicker to locate any particular recipe.

Ovens vary so cooking times may need to be adjusted accordingly.

I use garlic every time I use onions! However, the garlic is totally optional and can be left out.

Soups, Starters and Light Meals

Quick Potato Soup   8

Pastry Topping for Soup   8

Gazpacho   9

Spinach Soup   10

Pan Bagna   11

Soufflé Snack on Toast   12

Hot Tuna Open Sandwiches   12

Avocado and Bacon Rolls   13

Sunny Tomato Starter   13

Crab Salad on Poppadums   14

Smoked Trout Salad on Poppadums   15

Savoury Melon Marbles   16

Savoury Fresh Fruit Salad   17

Mediterranean Eggs   18

Tapenade   18

Special Party Dip 19

Scrambled Eggs with Smoked Salmon 20

Leek Omelette   20

Tofu Stir-fry   21

Spaghetti with Adare Cheese   22

Spaghetti with Green Vegetables   22

Tomato and Onion Rice   23

Cheesy Pancakes with Salsa   24

Salsa   24

Couscous with Courgettes   25

Black Pudding in Tapas Sauce

Quick Potato Soup

(Serves 4 - 6)

When I have almost nothing in the kitchen, I can still make a very tasty soup with potatoes, some onion and a little celery!

The gadget that cuts potatoes into chips is very handy when you want to dice potatoes in a hurry - once the potatoes are cut into the chip shapes, it only takes seconds to cut them into cubes.

2 medium/ large onions (175g/6oz), chopped
2 tablespoons oil
2 cloves garlic, chopped or crushed
2 big stalks celery, (110g/4oz), diced or chopped
450g (1 lb) potatoes, peeled and diced
900ml (1½ pt) chicken stock (OR use water and 1½ stock cubes)
Half a level teaspoon oregano or mixed herbs
Salt and freshly ground black pepper
1 - 2 tablespoons chopped fresh parsley
275ml (half pt) milk

Using a good sized, heavy-based saucepan, fry the chopped onions in the oil until soft, adding the garlic as it fries. Then add in the celery and potatoes. Fry together for a couple of minutes, without browning, and then pour in the stock (or water and stock cube). Add herbs and seasoning. Bring to the boil and then simmer gently, with the lid on, until the vegetables are tender.

The soup can be left with its 'chunky' texture or the vegetables can be very simply and quickly mashed - still in the soup saucepan- using a potato masher, (mash with gentle movements to avoid splashing). For a smoother texture, strain off the vegetables and buzz them in a food processor, returning the resulting purée to the soup.

To finish, add in the parsley and the milk, bring barely to the boil, simmer for a few minutes and serve.

Pastry Topping for Soup

Give a party finish to any soup by covering each serving bowl with puff pastry.

1 packet frozen puff pastry, thawed
6 ovenproof bowls, not too wide
1.1 litres (2 pt) soup of your choice
1 egg, beaten

Preheat Oven: 200°C, 400°F, Gas 6
Cooking Time: 15 - 20 minutes

Roll out pastry fairly thinly and cut about 2.5cm (1") larger than the top of the ovenproof bowls. Put the boiling hot soup into the bowls. Brush the outside rim of the bowls with the beaten egg. Place the circles of pastry over each bowl and press well to the outside rim. If necessary trim the edges to even the pastry. Stand the soup bowls on a baking tin and bake until the pastry is cooked to golden brown and puffed up nicely.

Gazpacho

(Serves 4 - 6)

There are many versions of this chilled Spanish soup, which originated in Andalucia. The name Gazpacho is thought to derive from the Arabic word for 'soaked bread', but bread is a minor ingredient, tomatoes being the main one. It requires no cooking at all, in fact it could be described as a 'liquid salad'! Tomato juice (tinned or bottled) provides the base and in this version the vegetables are buzzed in a food processor (or liquidizer) giving a nice texture and speckled colour.

2 slices of bread, crusts removed
425ml (three quarter pt) tomato juice
450g (1 lb) tomatoes
Half a red pepper, deseeded and chopped
Half a green pepper, deseeded and chopped
Third of a cucumber, peeled and chopped
2 - 3 cloves garlic, peeled and chopped
3 - 4 tablespoons (45 - 60ml) wine vinegar (red or white)
4 tablespoons (60ml) olive oil
Salt and freshly ground black pepper.

Note: The raw peppers have a strong flavour, if preferred chop finely and serve separately in little bowls, to be spooned over each serving of soup. Chopped hard-boiled egg can also be served in this fashion.

Put the bread into a bowl and pour the tomato juice over it.

Skin the tomatoes by immersing them in boiling water for about 1 minute then the skins will easily peel off. Also cut away the little stalk ends and chop roughly. Put the chopped tomatoes into a bowl and add in the peppers, cucumber and garlic.

Using a food processor, buzz these vegetables to a purée, in a few lots, adding in some of the tomato and bread mixture with each portion. The purée will not be totally smooth. Then, stir in the vinegar and oil and season to taste with the salt and pepper. Put into a serving bowl.

If the mixture seems a bit too thick, thin it by simply adding cold water. Chill the soup before serving.

Spinach Soup

Give yourself a special treat with this delicious, quickly-made soup. Use either fresh or frozen spinach. Fresh has a better flavour, though the frozen spinach makes a good substitute. As with most soups, it improves with reheating after a few hours (or the next day).

450g (1 lb) fresh spinach
Or   225 - 275g (8 - 10oz) frozen spinach
40g (1½ oz) butter
1 tablespoon olive oil
1 onion, finely chopped
2 cloves garlic, chopped or crushed
40g (1½ oz) flour (generous tablespoonful)
570 ml (1 pt) chicken stock (use a cube if necessary)
500ml (just under 1 pt) milk
Salt and freshly ground black pepper
1 bay leaf
1 whole clove (the apple tart kind !)
Generous pinches nutmeg
Few pinches of sugar

Prepare the spinach. Fresh spinach requires washing in plenty of fresh water, as it can be deceptively sandy and dusty. Cut away the stalks and any discoloured bits. Don't shake off the final, clean rinsing water. Put the wet spinach into a saucepan (without any other water), cover with a lid and cook for a few minutes until it goes limp and loses all its volume. Put into a food processor and buzz (or chop finely). Save any juices left in the saucepan.

If using frozen spinach allow it to thaw and chop finely.

Melt the butter with the olive oil in the (rinsed out) saucepan. Add in the onion and garlic and cook until soft and the mixture turns a pale golden colour. Stir in the flour, cook for a minute or two and then stir in the stock and the milk. Season with salt and pepper. Add in the spinach purée and juices, also the bay leaf and whole clove. Bring saucepan just to the boil and simmer gently with the lid loosely on for about 3 - 4 minutes. Stir in the nutmeg and sugar. (Lift out the bay leaf and whole clove.)

Serve with Croutons.

To make Croutons: Simply cut white bread into small cubes (shaking off the crumbs) and fry in a frying pan in shallow, hot oil. Drain on kitchen paper and season with salt and pepper.

Pan Bagna

A Mediterranean sandwich, native to Provence. A crusty French stick is filled with a type of salad Niçoise. Super for light lunch, lunch boxes or picnics. The real secret is to add good flavour to your olive oil.

110ml (4fl.oz) olive oil (flavoured, see below)
1 large French stick
2 - 3 hard-boiled eggs
Half small onion, cut in rings
1 - 2 sticks celery, chopped (optional)
Half a red or green pepper, cut in strips
3 nice red tomatoes, sliced
Salt and freshly ground black pepper
4 - 6 anchovy fillets (optional)
4 - 5 black or green olives (optional)
Lettuce leaves

Flavouring for the olive oil:
1 teaspoon fennel seeds, crushed
Salt and freshly ground black pepper
Half teaspoon oregano
1 clove garlic, crushed

Add all the flavouring ingredients to the oil. Leave to one side for at least 30 minutes (preferably overnight), then strain off the oil.

Slit the French stick in two and dribble a little of the flavoured oil onto the cut surfaces. Lay the slices of hard boiled eggs on one half of the bread with the thinly sliced onion on top. Scatter the celery and pepper strips over them and lay the sliced tomatoes on top. Dribble more of the olive oil all over the filling. Season with salt and pepper.

For the truly French touch, scatter the anchovy fillets and olives over the filling. Arrange the lettuce over everything. Cover with the other half of the bread. Wrap tightly in foil or cling film and leave to sit for at least an hour, allowing the flavours to mingle before serving.

Cooked spinach, with its wonderful velvety texture, flavoured with a hint of nutmeg and a little cream, is one of my favourite vegetables. Spinach is very rich in Vitamin A and also has generous amounts of calcium and iron. However, like rhubarb it contains oxalic acid, which tends to interfere with the absorption of these minerals and this is why it is not shovelled into children like it used to be years ago !

Spinach is available all the year round, when buying it fresh, it should have a bouncing, bright appearance and almost crunch and squeak when the leaves are gathered together. It is also available frozen.

Soufflé Snack on Toast

(Serves 1 - 2)

A beaten egg white added to the mixture gives a lovely fluffed up finish to this hearty snack. This amount covers two slices of toast which will make 1-2 servings depending on the size of the appetites !

1 large egg, separated
1 tablespoon mayonnaise
2 heaped tablespoons finely chopped cooked chicken
OR grated cheese
1 teaspoon finely chopped onion
2 teaspoons chopped parsley
Salt and freshly ground black pepper
2 slices toast

Separate the egg into two bowls. Stir the mayonnaise into the egg yolk, then add in the chicken (or cheese), onion and parsley. Season with the salt and pepper and mix well. Whisk the egg white until very stiff and then fold it through the egg yolk mixture. Spoon onto the toast. Cook under a medium grill until the mixture is 'set' and a nice golden colour. Serve with a little lettuce.

Hot Tuna Open Sandwiches

(Serves 4)

This makes a quick snack meal for four people.

Tuna is piled on sliced tomatoes on toast and grilled. (Tinned salmon can be used instead of tuna.)

3 - 4 tomatoes
4 slices toast, buttered
1 tin (approx. 200g) tuna, drained
1 tablespoon mayonnaise
Salt and freshly ground black pepper
A few pinches cayenne pepper (optional)
75g (3oz) grated cheese (cheddar and mozzarella)

If you like you can skin the tomatoes first by immersing them in boiling water for about 1 minute, then the skins will easily peel off. Slice the tomatoes and arrange in a layer on the toast. Place the tomato-covered toasts under a gentle grill to heat them up - without cooking - while you prepare the tuna mixture.

Mix the tuna with the mayonnaise season with salt, pepper and a few delicate pinches of the cayenne pepper. Spoon the mixture on top of the hot tomatoes. Scatter the cheese on top.

Grill under a moderate grill until the top is a lovely golden colour (ensure that the heat penetrates right through).

Avocado and Bacon rolls

Serve as a starter. Also makes a tasty breakfast or snack meal. Quartered avocados are wrapped in rashers and grilled. The sharp flavour of the sauce is an excellent accompaniment. Serves 2 as a starter, or 1 as a snack meal.

1 avocado
French mustard
4 back or streaky rashers
4 wooden cocktail sticks (optional)
A little oil

Sauce:
1 level teaspoon cornflour
Juice 1 large orange (75ml/3fl.oz)
1 teaspoon honey
1 - 2 teaspoons soy sauce
Freshly ground black pepper

Cut the avocado in half, then in quarters, removing the stone. Peel off the skin - treat gently. Spread a little mustard in the hole left by the stone. Wrap a rasher around each quarter, if necessary holding it in place with a cocktail stick. Brush all visible avocado with oil. Grill until rashers are crisp and brown all over.

Sauce: Blend the sauce ingredients together in a little saucepan and bring to the boil, stirring. Spoon over the cooked rolls.

Sunny Tomato Starter   (Serves 1 or more)

A very simple starter. Ideally, serve on small plain plates, with crusty bread to soak up the tasty juices !

For each serving allow:
1½ nice red tomatoes
3 - 4 green olives (stuffed with red peppers)
1 teaspoon finely chopped onion
Salt and freshly ground black pepper
Chopped fresh parsley
Tomato French dressing (page 101)

Cut the tomatoes into sixths or eighths, depending on size. Arrange them on the plates arranged like the spokes of a wheel, pointing out from the centre, with the olives in the middle. Scatter the onion on top. Dribble some of the dressing over them and season with pepper and a little salt. Scatter the parsley all over.

Crab Salad on Poppadums

(Serves 5 - 6)

A very attractive starter. Each portion is served on a crispy poppadum, decorated with sliced cherry tomatoes.

5 - 6 poppadums

Crab mixture:
2 tablespoons mayonnaise
110g (4oz) carton cottage cheese
1 tablespoon tomato ketchup
Dash tobasco sauce OR a few pinches of cayenne pepper
1 tablespoon finely chopped onion
1 tablespoon finely chopped fresh parsley
1 tablespoon green olives, chopped
350g (12oz) cooked frozen crab meat, defrosted (see note)
Squeeze of lemon juice
Salt and freshly ground black pepper, if necessary

To decorate:
Shredded lettuce
Paprika
Cherry tomatoes, halved
Slices of lemon

Note: If preferred use tinned crab meat (2 x 200g tins, drained)

To Cook Poppadums: Poppadums can be cooked in a jiffy in the microwave - with or without a light brushing of oil, just pop them in (one at a time) and allow 1 minute each on HIGH setting. They curl up into attractive 'bowl' shapes. (They can also be fried in oil, as per instructions on the packet.) If prepared in advance, wrap each one in cling film to keep crisp. Do not fill until just before serving, or they will go limp.

Put the mayonnaise and the cottage cheese into the food processor and buzz together until smooth (if no food processor is available, press the cottage cheese through a sieve). Put into a bowl and stir in all the other ingredients. Taste to check if seasoning is right. Cover and keep in the fridge until ready to serve.

To serve: Sit each poppadum on a little pile of shredded lettuce that peeps out from underneath. (This keeps the poppadums steady on the plate.) Spoon the crab mixture into the centre and sprinkle with light dusting of paprika. Decorate the crab mixture with the tomatoes and lemon.

Smoked Trout Salad on Poppadums (Serves 5 - 6)

This looks very pretty and can be mainly prepared in advance, though the assembly should only be done just before serving, otherwise the poppadums will lose their crispness.

5 - 6 poppadums - cooked as described in previous recipe (page 14)

75g (3oz) mangetout
Half medium cucumber, chopped
1 bunch spring onions (scallions), washed
2 kiwi fruit, peeled and chopped
Salt and freshly ground pepper
175g (6oz) smoked trout fillets

Dressing:
3 - 4 tablespoons mayonnaise
Juice half orange

To Decorate:
Shredded lettuce
Slices of lemon
Paprika
Fresh chopped parsley

If necessary put the mangetout into a bowl of cold water to refresh/crisp them. Drain, trim each end chop them in short lengths and put into a bowl. Add the chopped cucumber. (It is a personal preference whether you peel the cucumber or not, before chopping.) Thinly slice the spring onions and add with the kiwi to the bowl. Season with the salt and pepper. Add the dressing and toss.

Cut the smoked trout into bite sized chunks and gently stir through the salad.

To serve: Place some shredded lettuce on each small serving plate and sit a poppadum on top, allowing the lettuce to peep out around the edges. Spoon the salad mixture into the poppadum. Decorate with the lemon, paprika and chopped parsley.

Savoury Melon Marbles

(Serves 5 - 6)

Suitable as a starter or as a salad , this looks most attractive using two different coloured melons. Use a melon baller (potato-ball cutter), to scoop out the flesh into little marble (ball) shapes. To be economical, cut each shape really close to the previous one. Don't try to get perfect ball shapes or there will be far too much waste.

Half medium water melon (see note)
1 Galia melon
Half cucumber, optional
Small bunch spring onions (scallions)
1 tablespoon chopped fresh parsley
Salt and freshly ground black pepper
French dressing (page 100)

Note: When water melons are out of season substitute with another melon.

Scoop out the melon marbles (balls) as described above and put into a bowl. Remove and discard the seeds. Dice the cucumber and thinly slice the washed spring onions. Add to the melon with the parsley. Season with salt and pepper. When ready to serve add enough of the French dressing to moisten.

Serve in individual little bowls (or wine glasses), decorated with a little extra chopped parsley.

If preparing this salad in advance, don't add the dressing, as juice will continue to drain out of the melons, thus diluting the dressing. Before serving drain off this excess juice and then add the dressing.

In Europe, the high season and place for water-melons , is August 10th, in Florence (according to Jane Grigson in her Fruit Cookery Book). This day is, by repute, the hottest day of the year. It is also the feast day of San Lorenzo, the patron saint of cooks, who met his end, grilled over charcoal on a gridiron ! When ordered by the Roman Emperor Valerian, to produce the riches of the church, San Lorenzo gathered together the sick and handicapped, explaining that these were the riches of the church. This obviously was not what the emperor had in mind ! With all that heat no wonder the cooling, juicy water-melons seem so attractive.

Water-melons are the largest of all melons, though nowadays smaller more manageable sized ones are available. The dark, glossy skin conceals magic, red coloured flesh, speckled with black seeds, that is really juicy when fresh, though it becomes woolly and dry look-ing when stale.

Savoury Fresh Fruit Salad (Serves 5 - 6)

Normally associated with desserts, a fresh fruit salad dressed with a French dressing makes a really good starter. It is also excellent as a side salad. If made in advance it can get quite juicy , but use crusty bread to soak up all the delicious juices.

The choice of fruit used can vary, depending on availability, but these are the ones I like to use:

1 eating apple, chopped (not peeled)
1 pear, peeled and chopped
OR 1 mango peeled and chopped
2 oranges peeled and cut in juicy segments (see note)
2 nectarines, chopped
2 bananas, peeled and chopped
110g (4oz) grapes, halved and pips removed
4 - 6 strawberries, chopped (optional)
Small bunch of spring onions , washed and chopped
French dressing (see page 100)
4 - 6 leaves of mint, chopped (optional)
OR 1 tablespoon chopped parsley

Mix all the salad ingredients together in a bowl. Add in enough of the dressing to coat the fruit and scatter the fresh mint or parsley on top.

Note: To segment an orange; Peel the orange with a sharp knife, removing all the pith, so just the flesh shows. Carefully cut out each segment of orange from between the membranes (thin inner skin). Remove any pips.

Mediterranean Eggs

These are eggs "poached" in a full pan of Mediterranean type vegetables and are wonderfully tasty. Serve with wholemeal or crusty bread.

1 small/ medium onion
1 - 2 cloves garlic, chopped
2 - 3 tablespoonfuls of olive oil
2 medium peppers, red or green
1 medium courgette, chopped
3 tomatoes, chopped
Salt and freshly ground black pepper
A few pinches of oregano or herbes de Provence
3 - 4 eggs
1 tablespoon chopped fresh parsley

Thinly slice and chop the onion and fry it, with the garlic, in the oil until they are soft. Deseed and chop the peppers and add to the pan. Cover with a lid. This keeps in the steam and helps to cook the peppers more quickly. After a couple of minutes add the courgette and tomatoes. Season with salt and pepper, and flavour with herbs. Remove lid and continue cooking for a few minutes until the vegetables are almost soft. Make 3 or 4 hollows into the 'bed' of vegetables and break an egg into each one. Season each with a little pepper and salt. Replace the lid and simmer gently until the eggs are set and white on top, but still soft inside. Scatter with chopped parsley. To serve, lift out each egg together with all its surrounding vegetables. Serve with crusty bread.

Tapenade

A speciality from Provence, this is a delicious, dark, pungent paste or spread. Speckled grey/black in colour, it is made with black olives, capers and anchovies. These are not everyday ingredients I know, but it is delicious on toast, crusty French bread or crispy water biscuits and served as 'finger food'.

1 tin anchovy fillets
A little milk
110g (4oz) black olives, stones removed
110g (4oz) capers, drained
1 teaspoon French mustard
Freshly ground black pepper
Quarter teaspoon nutmeg
150ml (quarter pt) olive oil
1 - 2 cloves crushed garlic (optional)

Drain the oil from the anchovy fillets and steep them in a little milk for about 10 minutes to reduce the saltiness.

Put the olives into a food processor with the capers and mustard. Season with the pepper and flavour with the nutmeg. Drain the milk off the anchovies and add them to the food processor. Buzz everything together and as it buzzes, gradually dribble in the olive oil. The crushed garlic can be added with the oil if you are using it. Cover well, it will keep in the fridge for a few weeks.

The tapenade tastes particularly good with eggs, so try spreading it on egg sandwiches.

Special Party Dip (Makes 275ml/half pt)

A delicious dip with unexpected ingredients. I evolved this recipe for those who must avoid, not only high fat foods, but also dairy products. The base is a purée of cauliflower and in case you throw up your hands in horror, let me assure you that it is very hard to detect it.

1 medium head of cauliflower
570ml (1 pt) water
1 chicken stock cube
Fillets of smoked trout (about 110g/4oz)
1 tablespoon mayonnaise (low fat)
1 teaspoon English mustard
Salt and freshly ground black pepper

Break the cauliflower into florets and cut a deep cross into each stalk end (to speed up cooking). Choose a wide-based saucepan (so the florets will fit in a single layer). Put in the water and stock cube, cover and bring to the boil. When dissolved, drop in the florets. Cover and cook until soft and tender, but be careful not to over-cook. Drain well.

Buzz the cooked cauliflower, in two or three lots in a food processor. Add the smoked trout, mayonnaise and mustard with the last portion. Mix everything together and season lightly if necessary.

Serve with crudités.

The Mediterranean diet is constantly being held out to us as an example of healthy eating. The key factor, according to the dieticians, is that fruit and vegetables feature very strongly in Mediterranean cookery and also olive oil (high in monounsaturates) is the main source of fat. To emulate their diet, we do not have to eat exactly the same vegetables as they do, our own native vegetables are also excellent. The main thing is to include much more vegetables and fruit in our daily diet.

Scrambled Eggs with Smoked Salmon

(Serves 1 or more)

The secret of a nice moist scrambled egg, is to take the saucepan off the heat before all of the egg mixture has quite set, the residual heat finishes the cooking. Serve immediately.

Allow per person:
Approx. 25g (1 oz) smoked salmon
A little lemon juice
1 - 2 eggs
Half tablespoon milk
Salt and freshly ground black (or white) pepper
Small knob of butter
1 slice buttered toast or cooked poppadum

To decorate:
Chopped fresh chives, chopped fresh parsley or sprig of fresh dill

Cut the smoked salmon into little strips and dribble the lemon juice over them.

Break the eggs into a bowl. Add the milk, salt and pepper and whisk until mixed, without making them very frothy. Melt the butter in a saucepan and stir in the egg mixture . Cook over a moderate heat, stirring gently, until almost cooked, then lift off the heat. Stir in the smoked salmon (cook a little more if necessary). Serve on hot toast or poppadum. Scatter generously with chopped fresh chives or parsley, or a sprig of fresh dill.

Leek Omelette

(Serves 3 - 4)

Like a Spanish tortilla, the top of the cooked omelette is browned under the grill. Leeks and eggs are great together. Makes a marvellous lunch, brunch or anytime meal.

450g (1 lb) leeks
25g (1oz) butter
1 tablespoon oil
50ml (2fl.oz) water
Salt and freshly ground black pepper
Juice half lemon
6 eggs
3 tablespoons milk
50g (2oz) grated cheese (preferably gruyère)
Chopped fresh parsley

Top and tail the leeks, wash thoroughly and then slice thinly. Melt the butter with the oil in a pan. Add in the leeks and water. Fry gently until soft and boil off any remaining water. Season with salt and pepper and stir in the lemon juice.

Meanwhile, beat the eggs in a bowl with the milk, pepper and salt. Pour this over the softened leeks in the pan and shake gently together. Sprinkle the cheese on top. Cook over a gentle heat until the mixture is almost set and the underneath is browned. Place the pan under the grill (protect the handle) and cook until the top is golden. Leave the omelette to sit on the pan for about 5 minutes before sliding it off the pan onto a plate. Scatter with the chopped parsley. Serve hot or cold.

Tofu Stir-Fry (Serves 3 -4)

Tofu is a pale soft cheese-like substance, made from soya beans, which contains a good quality protein. Thus it is often used as a meat substitute. It has very little flavour. Tofu, flavoured with soy sauce is excellent in a stir-fry.

175g (6oz) Tofu, cut in chunks
A little soy sauce
A little oil, for frying
1 small onion, thinly sliced
1 - 2 cloves garlic, crushed
110g (4oz) mushrooms sliced
75 - 110g (3 - 4oz) sweetcorn (thawed)
1 red or yellow pepper, deseed and cut in strips
50 - 110g (2 - 4oz) mangetout, cut in short lengths
3 tablespoons pineapple chunks
1 teaspoon grated fresh root ginger (optional)

Sauce:
150ml (quarter pt) pineapple juice (from the tin of pineapple chunks)
2 - 3 tablespoons soy sauce
1 heaped teaspoon cornflour
Salt and freshly ground black pepper

Steep the tofu and the soy sauce together for at least 30 minutes and then drain off any excess sauce.

Prepare all the vegetables and mix the sauce ingredients together in a jug.

Heat the oil in a wok or frying pan. Fry the onion, garlic and mushrooms, then add in the sweetcorn, pepper and mangetout, and cook tossing constantly until the vegetables are half tender. Add the pineapple chunks, ginger, tofu and the sauce mixture to the wok/pan. Bring to the boil, constantly stirring and continue cooking over a gentle heat until the vegetables are bite tender. Serve with rice or noodles.

Spaghetti with Adare Cheese

(Serves 4)

A blend of Italian and Irish cuisine. The Adare cheese with its lovely ham and cheese flavour, makes a filling spaghetti dish, that is cooked in minutes.

450g (1 lb) spaghetti
Chicken stock cube
1 tablespoon olive oil
1 - 2 cloves garlic, crushed
75ml (3fl.oz) fresh cream
110 - 175g (4 - 6oz) Adare cheese, grated
Salt and freshly ground black pepper

Cook the spaghetti in plenty of boiling water to which a chicken stock cube has been added. When bite-tender, drain the spaghetti.

Put the oil into the rinsed out saucepan and gently fry the garlic until soft. Then add in the drained spaghetti and pour in the cream. Add the cheese and toss everything together over a gentle heat, seasoning with salt and pepper. Serve immediately.

Spaghetti with Green Vegetables

(Serves 4)

A fresh tasting spaghetti dish, cooked in minutes. It is worth buying freshly grated Parmesan cheese for better flavour.

350g (12oz) spaghetti
Vegetable stock cube
2 - 3 tablespoons olive oil
1 small onion, chopped
1 - 2 cloves garlic, crushed
1 - 2 leeks, thinly sliced
2 sticks celery, thinly sliced
1 courgette, chopped
50g (2oz) cooked peas (optional)
1 small eating apple, chopped (optional)
Salt and freshly ground black pepper
Quarter teaspoon oregano
2 tablespoons of chopped fresh parsley

To serve: Freshly grated Parmesan cheese

Cook the spaghetti in plenty of boiling water, to which the stock has been added. When bite-tender, drain the spaghetti.

Rinse out the saucepan, put the oil in it and gently fry the onion and garlic until soft. Then add in the leek and other vegetables and apple. Season with the salt and pepper and oregano. Cover with a lid and cook gently, stirring or tossing frequently for a few minutes until the vegetables are tender. Add in the spaghetti and toss with the vegetables.

Serve scattered with chopped parsley and lots of Parmesan cheese.

Tomato and Onion rice

Moist and flavoursome.

350g (12oz) long grained rice
1 tin chopped tomatoes
Chicken stock
1 - 2 medium onions, sliced
2 tablespoons olive oil
1 - 2 cloves garlic, chopped
Salt and freshly ground black pepper
Quarter teaspoon mixed herbs
2 tablespoons chopped fresh parsley

Measure the volume of rice in a cup or measure. Then measure the volume of the tin of chopped tomatoes. Add enough chicken stock to the tomatoes, so together they measure two and a half times the volume of the rice.

Using a heavy-bottomed saucepan, fry the onion in the oil with the garlic until soft. Then add in the rice and stir for a minute or two over the heat. Then add in all the remaining ingredients (retain half the parsley). Bring to the boil and cover the saucepan with a lid and simmer very gently until the rice is tender, by which time it will have absorbed all the liquid. Takes about 25 minutes for white rice and 35 minutes for whole grain rice. Check occasionally, to ensure it doesn't cook dry. If by any chance the rice is not cooked and all the liquid has been absorbed, then add a little boiling water and continue cooking.

Serve with remaining parsley sprinkled on top.

Cheesy Pancake with Salsa (Serves 3 - 4)

These cheese filled pancakes are so simple and very tasty. Served with salsa they make a light or substantial meal - depending on how many you eat ! This quantity of batter will give about 5 - 8 pancakes depending on what size you make them.

Basic pancake batter:
110g (4oz) flour
1 large egg
275ml (half) pt milk

Put everything into a food processor and buzz for a minute to make a smooth batter OR put the flour into a mixing bowl, adding in the egg and milk. Using a wire whisk stir well and then whisk for a couple of minutes to make the batter. Leave the batter to stand for at least 15 minutes to allow the flour grains absorb the liquid and make it more creamy and easier to handle.

Cheese filling:
Approx. 110g (4oz) grated cheese (cheddar and mozzarella)

Salsa:
See recipe below.

Have cheese filling and salsa ready before frying the pancakes.

To fry pancakes: Not much fat is required. For convenience I use a big lump of margarine, half covered in foil. Then, before the frying of each pancake, I rub the hot pan with the margarine. (The foil wrapping prevents my fingers getting messy. I stand the margarine on a little saucer to catch the drips.)

Pour the batter (2 - 4 tablespoons) into the pan, tilting the pan to spread the batter out. Fry over a fairly hot heat and when browned underneath, turn over to cook the other side. Immediately, scatter some grated cheese over the top, so that as the underneath of the pancake cooks, the cheese will be getting hot and starting to melt. Season lightly with freshly grated black pepper and a little salt.

When the underneath is cooked simply roll up the pancake and keep warm until they are all ready.

Serve with the salsa.

Salsa

Delightful fresh tasting sauce made with raw ingredients.

3 nice red tomatoes, skinned
Quarter - half small red pepper
10cm/4" piece of cucumber (peeled)
Quarter of a small onion
Salt and freshly ground black pepper
A few pinches cayenne pepper
A few pinches of sugar
1 tablespoon finely chopped parsley
1 - 2 teaspoons of vinegar (preferably wine vinegar)

Cut the tomatoes in half and scoop out the seeds. Roughly chop the flesh. Also roughly chop the pepper, cucumber and the onion. Put these into a food processor and give them a short buzz to chop them finely. Season with salt, pepper, cayenne pepper and sugar. Stir in the parsley and vinegar. (If no food processor is available, chop everything finely.

Couscous with Courgettes (Serves 3)

Couscous, found in many north African dishes, is actually a type of pasta. Like bulgar, it needs rehydrating, soaking the fine 'grains' in water (or stock) for about 30 minutes during which time they swell up considerably. Despite the fact that many recipes use water for soaking the couscous, I find the resulting flavour rather 'flat' and much prefer to use a stock. The vegetables can be varied to taste.

110g (4oz) couscous (quick cooking)
275ml (half pt) chicken stock (boiling)
1 - 2 tablespoons oil
1 leek, medium-size, thinly sliced
Half courgette (about 75g/3oz), chopped
1 - 2 cloves garlic, crushed
Salt and freshly ground black pepper
1 generous tablespoon chopped fresh parsley.

Put the couscous into a bowl, cover with the boiling stock and allow to soak for about 5 minutes. Then, top, tail and wash the leek and slice thinly.

Put the oil into the saucepan and fry the leek, courgette and the garlic until soft. Add the couscous into a saucepan with the courgette and stir together over the heat. Cover and cook for a few minutes (don't let it stick). Season to taste with the salt and pepper. Stir in the parsley. Serve hot or cold.

Black Pudding in Tapas Sauce

(Serves 3 as a light meal or 6 as tapas)

The Spanish enjoy black pudding just as we do and often serve it with this Tapas Sauce. The sauce can be used with other foods.

It is worth noting that black pudding is a very rich source of iron.

Sauce:
1 small chopped onion
1 tablespoon olive oil
1 clove garlic, crushed
275ml (half pt) tomato juice
Salt and freshly ground black pepper
Generous pinches of cayenne pepper
Pinches of nutmeg
Half teaspoon oregano
1 - 2 tablespoons vinegar
1 teaspoon sugar
6 green olives, chopped (optional)
2 heaped teaspoons cornflour
350g (12oz) black pudding
A little oil for frying

Sauce: Using a medium sized saucepan, fry the onion in the olive oil until soft, adding in the garlic. Draw off the heat and pour in the tomato juice. Season with the salt, pepper and cayenne pepper. Add the nutmeg, oregano, vinegar, sugar olives and the cornflour (blended with a little water). Bring the sauce to the boil to thicken. Serve hot or cold.

Cut the black pudding into slices and fry both sides in a little oil until cooked through. Drain on a paper towel and serve with sauce poured over.

Dress each serving with a little green salad.

Many customs can be very wise. For example, in many Mediterranean countries it is the custom to serve little snacks with drinks. Alcohol is one of the very few substances that is absorbed directly into the system through the walls of the stomach. If the stomach contains some food, the absorption of the alcohol is slowed down. Fatty foods are best because they take the longest time to digest. Serving "finger food" at cocktail parties is based on the same principle. The Spanish serve tapas in their bars. They can be as uncomplicated as a dish of olives or nuts, or they can be as elaborate as little meals. Larger bars often serve as many as twenty or thirty different tapas. Frequently, people eat a variety of tapas instead of their evening meal. Tapas recipes are also suitable to serve as starters or as light meals without a drink in sight!

Fish

Cod Fillets in Cider Sauce

(Serves 4 - 5)

It is all very well for the French to use lots of wine in their cooking, they can pop round to their local shop and buy it for next to nothing!

Looking for a cheaper substitute, I find that dry cider does quite a good job.

4 - 5 pieces of cod fillet (150g /5oz each)

Sauce:
3 - 4 streaky rashers, chopped
1 - 2 tablespoons oil
1 small onion, chopped
1 clove garlic, chopped
110g (4oz) courgettes, diced OR tender celery stalks, chopped
350ml (12fl.oz) dry cider
Salt and freshly ground pepper
Generous pinches of thyme (or mixed herbs)
2 rounded teaspoons cornflour
1 - 2 tablespoons mayonnaise
1 tablespoon chopped fresh parsley

Choose nice chunky pieces of cod, rinse them under the cold tap and pat dry. Leave to one side and make the sauce.

Fry the rashers in a small drop of oil and when crispy lift out. Wipe out the salty fat from the pan and put in fresh oil. Fry the onion and garlic until soft, then add in the courgettes and fry until lightly browned (if using celery it need not be browned). Add in the cider. Season with salt, pepper and thyme. Bring to the boil and simmer briskly for a few minutes to soften the vegetables and boil off the alcohol. Blend the cornflour with a little drop of water and then stir in the mayonnaise. Stir this into the cider mixture. Bring to the boil, stirring to thicken. Put the fish into the sauce spooning some over the top of the fillets. Partly cover and simmer gently until cooked through, (about 6 - 10 minutes). Serve scattered with the parsley.

Cheesy Fish

(Serves 3 - 4)

The fish is cooked on a bed of fried mushrooms and then topped with some grated cheese and grilled. Choose nice fillets of cod or haddock.

1 medium onion, chopped
2 - 3 tablespoons oil
1 clove garlic, crushed
225g (8oz) mushrooms, sliced
Salt and freshly ground black pepper
Pinches of oregano
4 - 8 olives chopped (optional)
2 - 4 tablespoons cream (optional)
450g (1 lb) fish fillets
110g (4oz) grated cheese, (cheddar and mozzarella)

Fry the onion in the oil until soft, adding in the garlic. Then add in the mushrooms. Fry until they become soft. Season with the salt and pepper and flavour with the oregano. Stir in the olives and cream if using them. Lay the fish fillets on top. Season fillets with salt and pepper. Scatter with the grated cheese. Cover with a lid and simmer gently until the fish is almost cooked (6-10 minutes depending on the thickness of the fillets). Then place under a hot grill until the cheese turns golden brown.

Cod and Bacon Bites

(Serves 4)

Nice fat, bite-sized chunks of cod are wrapped in rashers, threaded onto skewers and grilled or barbecued until cooked through. For extra flavour spread a little pesto or mayonnaise on each piece of fish before rolling them up. Thread each one onto its own wooden cocktail stick and serve as "finger food".

450g (1 lb) cod, with the skin removed, cut into 10 - 12 bite-sized chunks
A little pesto or mayonnaise
10 - 12 small streaky rashers
Metal or wooden skewers (see note)

Note: if using wooden skewers or even wooden cocktail sticks, steep them in cold water for at least 30 minutes beforehand to prevent them burning.

Spread each piece of cod with a little pesto or mayonnaise. Wrap a rasher round each chunk of fish, (if the rashers are too long, trim them), and push onto skewers or cocktail sticks. Grill, turning occasionally during cooking. Takes about 10 - 15 minutes to cook through.

Norwegian Cod

Fillets of cod are cooked on a bed of vegetables that includes celery and cooking apples. The combination of flavours is particularly nice.

Half way through cooking the fish is turned over to reveal the less well-done side underneath. This is spread with mayonnaise and finished under the grill. The tasty vegetables are served with the fish. Accompany with potatoes or crusty bread.

1 large onion, chopped
1 tablespoon oil
1 small clove garlic, crushed
175g (6oz) celery, chopped (see note)
1 medium cooking apple, peeled and chopped
2 - 3 tomatoes, skinned and chopped
200ml (8fl.oz) stock (OR use half a fish or chicken stock cube)
1 heaped teaspoon cornflour
Freshly ground pepper
A little salt if necessary
A few pinches oregano
2 tablespoons chopped fresh parsley
350g - 450g (¾ - 1 lb) cod fillets
A little oil
1 - 2 tablespoons mayonnaise

Note: Choose the more tender sticks from the centre of the head of celery

Using a wide frying pan, fry the onion in the oil, adding the garlic and celery. When soft add the cooking apple and tomatoes. Blend the stock into the corn-flour and pour over the vegetables. Add seasoning, herbs and half the parsley. Bring to the boil to thicken. Taste and add salt if necessary.

The fillet of fish can be left in one piece or cut into three or four pieces. Place it skin side upwards, on top of the hot vegetables. Cover with a lid (or foil), and simmer gently for about 6 minutes. Then, gently turn the fish so the flesh side is facing upwards, and spread with mayonnaise. Place the whole pan under the grill, and cook for a few minutes until the fish is cooked through.

Serve sprinkled with the remaining parsley.

Fresh root ginger has a wonderful flavour. Choose it as fresh as possible, avoiding with-ered roots. Peel off the outside skin and slice or grate as required. Don't let leftover gin-ger wither up in the fridge - if not using it, grate the ginger and wrap small amounts in cling film, then freeze it ready for use.

Salmon with Tomatoes and Ginger (Serves 4 - 5)

The ginger and orange makes a lovely sweet sauce which is unusual with fish. It is also very good with chicken (see page 59).

450 - 700g (1 - 1½ lb) salmon fillets

Sauce:
2 cloves garlic, crushed
1 level tablespoon grated fresh root ginger
1 tablespoon oil
3 - 4 spring onions (scallions), chopped thinly
5 - 6 tomatoes, skinned and chopped
3 rounded teaspoons cornflour
Juice 3 large oranges (approx. 250ml/ 9fl.oz)
2 - 3 teaspoons vinegar
1 tablespoon soy sauce (light flavour)
A few pinches sugar
Quarter teaspoon oregano
Freshly ground pepper and salt

To serve: 1 tablespoon chopped fresh parsley

Preheat Oven: 190°C, 375°F, Gas 5.

Cooking Time: About 15 minutes

Lightly oil an ovenproof dish and put it into the oven to heat.

Wash the fish and pat dry, leave to one side.

Meanwhile make the sauce: Using a saucepan, gently fry the garlic and ginger in the oil. After a minute or two add the spring onions, and the tomatoes. Simmer together for 2 - 3 minutes.

Put the cornflour into a little bowl and stir in the orange juice, vinegar and soy sauce. Flavour with the sugar and oregano. Season with the pepper and a little salt. Pour into the saucepan with the vegetables and bring to the boil, stirring, until it thickens.

Put the fish fillets into the hot dish . Pour the sauce over and cover loosely with some foil. Cook in the oven until the flesh flakes easily with a fork.

When serving, scatter generously with the chopped fresh parsley.

Hungarian Fish Salad

(Serves 4 - 5)

Although it has no coastline, Hungary has one of the largest inland lakes in Europe and so fish feature frequently on Hungarian menus. The fresh water fish they use can be substituted with sea fish as in this recipe.

This looks most attractive with the strong red and green coloured peppers contrasting with the white fish.

450g (1 lb) white fish fillets (cod or haddock etc.)
Fish (or chicken) stock, (use a cube if necessary)
French dressing (see page 100)
2 green peppers
3 tomatoes
Third of a cucumber
1 small bunch of spring onions (scallions)
Salt and freshly ground black pepper
2 teaspoons paprika
Quarter teaspoon cayenne pepper
Chopped fresh parsley

To serve: mayonnaise

Poach the fish very gently in the stock (for flavour). Lift out and remove the skin and bones. Sprinkle some of the dressing on the fish and allow it to cool.

Chop the peppers, tomatoes, cucumber and spring onions. (For this recipe I do not skin the peppers as their sharp flavour provides good contrast.)

Mix the vegetables together in a bowl and season with the pepper and salt and add in the paprika and cayenne pepper. Stir in some French dressing and toss together. Finally mix the chunks of fish gently through.

Serve on a flat dish and scatter a little parsley on top. Accompany with mayonnaise.

Variation: Include **1 fresh mango,** peeled and chopped, mixed in with the salad. It adds nice flavour and colour.

Picture opposite: Mediterranean Eggs

Overleaf Left: Spaghetti with Green Vegetables

Overleaf Right: Roast Chicken Layered Loaf

Fillets of Trout with Pesto and Prawns   (Serves 4 - 5)

A super combination of flavours! Ready-made pesto can be bought in jars. The fish can be cooked in a covered frying pan, or in the oven. Mushrooms can be used instead of prawns.

4 - 5 fillets of rainbow trout.
About 4 - 5 teaspoons pesto sauce
1 tin (200g) prawns, drained (see note)
Salt and freshly ground black pepper if necessary

To serve:
Chopped fresh parsley
Paprika

Note: Tinned prawns are more economical to use, but for a special occasion use freshly cooked prawns.

For best results, remove the small little bones from the trout fillets and then skin the fillets (directions on page 39).

Place the prepared fillets on a board, skinned side upwards. Spread a generous teaspoon of pesto on each fillet. Arrange the drained prawns in a little mound on the thick end of each fillet. Fold the narrow end right over the prawns. (The prawns will be peeping out, because the narrow end is not wide enough to cover them.) Lift onto a lightly oiled frying pan and cover with a lid (or large piece of foil). Cook at a gentle simmer until fish is done, about 8 - 10 minutes.

Serve, scattered with chopped parsley and paprika.

To cook in oven: If preferred, place prepared fish on a greased dish and bake for about 10 - 20 minutes in a moderately hot oven (190°C, 375°F, gas 5) until cooked.

Alternative to the prawns: Fry **150g (5oz) mushrooms, thinly sliced** in a tablespoon of oil until nice and tasty. Then place on the trout fillets instead of the prawns.

Picture Opposite: Black Pudding and Tapas Sauce, Pastry Topping on Soup, Avocado Rolls, Smoked Trout Salad on Poppadums

Fresh Salmon and Pesto Quiche

(Serves 5 - 6)

Ideal for so many occasions - light lunch, supper time or, if served in narrow wedges, it is also suitable as a starter.

The pastry base: You can use frozen pastry (either shortcrust or puff) or for a special occasion try this -

Parmesan Pastry:
150g (5oz) flour
50g (2oz) ground almonds
25g (1oz) Parmesan cheese, grated
Salt and freshly ground black pepper
75g (3oz) margarine or butter
About 3 tablespoons water

The filling:
1 onion, chopped
2 tablespoons oil
1 - 2 cloves garlic, crushed
175g (6 oz) mushrooms, sliced
75g (3oz) courgette, cut into small cubes (optional)
Juice half lemon
225g (8 oz) fresh salmon fillets
2 - 3 teaspoons pesto
2 large eggs
2 tablespoons mayonnaise
About 175ml (6fl.oz) milk
Salt and freshly ground black pepper
1 - 2 tablespoons finely chopped fresh parsley

Tin: Sandwich tin or flan dish - 23cm (9") in diameter. Grease lightly.

Preheat Oven: 200°C, 400°F, Gas 6.

Cooking Time: Cook for about 40 minutes. If necessary - reduce the heat during the cooking - but try to keep cooking at the higher temperature for as long as possible, to ensure that the bottom of the pastry is cooked.

Pastry: Mix together the first three ingredients, season with salt and pepper. Add the margarine (cold from the fridge), cut in lumps, and rub in until like breadcrumbs. (The food processor is excellent for doing this, but only buzz for a few seconds at a time or else the mixture is liable to lose it's crumbliness, or worse still, turn into a lump of dough, before you have added in the water.) Transfer the "crumbly" mixture to a bowl. Add barely enough water to bind the dry ingredients together. (Use a fork for mixing, to mash and squeeze the water effectively through the flour.) Gather the pastry into a ball and leave to one side (covered) for about 5 minutes to relax before rolling out. No need to chill this pastry in the fridge. It is easy to handle.

Roll out and line the tin with the pastry.

Filling: Lightly fry the onion in the oil until soft, adding in the garlic. Lift out with a perforated spoon and spread over the base of the pastry case. Then fry the mushrooms until they too are soft and flavoursome and add to the onions. Do the same with the courgette. Squeeze the lemon juice over these vegetables.

Skin the salmon, remove any little bones, and cut into bite-sized chunks. Spread just a little bit of pesto on each chunk and place on top of the vegetable filling, settling them down into the filling, rather than standing too high on top.

Whisk together the eggs and the mayonnaise until smooth, then mix in the milk, salt, pepper and parsley. Pour into the pastry case and bake until golden brown on top and the mixture is set.

Removing Little Bones from Fish Fillets

Even in filleted fish you can still find little small bones, which, for many, spoil the pleasure of eating fish.

It is quite an easy task to remove these bones, especially in larger fillets e.g. cod or salmon. Lay the fillet, skin side down on a board and run your fingertips along the flesh and you will feel the sharp points of little bones in a straight row. These can easily be pulled out with a little pliers (or cut away). However, in sea trout and especially rainbow trout, the bones are very fine and close together. The easiest way to remove them is to cut a very narrow wedge of the flesh with the bones included in it. This 'wedge' can then be pulled out and discarded. (The closer you are able to cut beside these little bones, on each side, the less flesh will be wasted.) Double check with your fingertips that no bones have been left behind. Alternatively - ask your fishmonger to do all this for you !

To Skin a Fillet

This is easily done because the skin is tough. Just place the fillet, skin side down, with the narrow tail end pointing towards you. Using a sharp knife, separate the flesh from the skin at the narrow point and then holding that bit of skin in your left hand continue cutting between the skin and flesh, working away from you. Keep the blade of the knife angled slightly downwards towards the skin, since it doesn't cut easily. The flesh will be easily separated from the skin. (If skinning small rectangular pieces of fish fillets, simply start at one corner to separate the flesh from the skin.)

Cut off any fins, including the hard wedge of flesh to which the fins are attached.

Fillets of Sea Trout Stuffed with Bacon and Mushrooms

(Serves 6)

Two full fillets of sea trout are sandwiched together with this delicious stuffing in the middle. As all the bones are removed it is very easy to serve. Fillets of a small salmon could be used instead.

Even though the ingredients are chopped before frying, the stuffing ingredients are then buzzed in a food processor to chop them even more finely - almost like breadcrumbs.

For 3 servings use half quantities

Fish:
2 fillets sea trout , about 500g (18oz) each
Sprig of fennel (optional)

Bacon and Mushroom Stuffing:
225g (8oz) lean rashers
2 - 3 tablespoons olive oil
1 small onion, chopped
1 - 2 cloves garlic, crushed
225g (8oz) mushrooms, sliced
Salt and freshly ground black pepper
Generous pinches of nutmeg
Generous pinches of herbes de Provence (or oregano)
1 teaspoon finely grated lemon peel

Preheat Oven: 180°C, 350°F, Gas 4.

Cooking Time: About 20 - 30 minutes.

Make up the stuffing: Fry the onion and garlic together in 2 tablespoons of the oil. Add the mushrooms and fry until they soften, then lift out everything with a perforated spoon. Buzz this mixture in a food processor to chop finely - almost like breadcrumbs. Put into bowl. Next fry the rashers. When cooked drain them on a paper towel. Buzz them in a food processor, to chop them very finely. Put into the bowl with the onions and mushrooms. Add the rest of the stuffing ingredients and mix together.

Prepare the fish: Remove the little bones from the fillets (see directions on page 39). Also cut off any fins, but do **not** remove the skin.

Put a large piece of foil (shiny side facing up) on a baking tin and place a piece of baking parchment on top. Brush the centre with a little oil. Place one fillet, skin side downwards on the oiled parchment. Spread the stuffing on top in an even layer. Lay the second fillet on top (skin side upwards). Brush with a little oil, put the fennel beside the fish and season with salt and pepper. Then fold over the parchment and foil to completely wrap up the fish, and hold in the tasty juices which come out during cooking.

Bake in a moderate oven until cooked - about 20 - 30 minutes. It is hard to be exact about the time, because the thickness of the fish fillets vary. To test, gently lift the thicker end of the fillet to check underneath OR make a little hole in the centre of the thickest flesh and check if the colour is the same right through. Avoid overcooking (as it will continue to cook while resting).

Like a meat roast, the fish is best left standing for 10 - 15 minutes before serving. Keep warm (I leave the foil on top and cover with a tea towel). Serve in generous slices.

If liked the juices from around the fish can be added to a **white sauce,** along with a **spoon of lemon juice (or mayonnaise)** and served with the fish. (The recipe for Lemon and Parsley Sauce on page 45 is suitable to use, substitute the juices from the tinned salmon in the recipe with the juices from the baked sea trout.)

Rainbow Trout Stuffed with Bacon and Mushrooms (Serves 6)

The smaller fillets of rainbow trout can be used instead of the sea trout. The stuffing used in the previous recipe is enough to make three 'sandwiches' from **6 fillets of rainbow trout.** Wrap in parchment and foil and cook in the same way, for about 15 - 20 minutes until cooked.

Grilled Fillets of Rainbow Trout (Serves 1 or more)

Delicious and really simple, other fish fillets can be cooked this way.

Per serving:
1 fillet of rainbow trout
Half tablespoon mayonnaise
1 level tablespoon flaked almonds

Remove the bones from the fillet (see instructions page 39).

Remove the wire grid from the grill pan and just use the flat grill pan (if liked, line it with foil) and brush with oil (to prevent the fish sticking). Heat the pre-pared grill pan until piping hot, before putting in the fish (skin side down), as this speeds up the cooking. Spread the mayonnaise on the fish , grill for about 5 minutes and then scatter the almonds over the fish and grill for a further few minutes until golden. The precise cooking time depends on the thickness of the fish.

Rolled Fillets of Rainbow Trout

(Serves 1 or more)

The skinned fillets are spread with a little mayonnaise, rolled up and then baked in the oven. Lovely and moist.

Per serving:
1 fillet rainbow trout
2 teaspoons mayonnaise
Salt and freshly ground pepper

Preheat Oven: 190°C, 375°F, Gas 5.

Cooking Time: About 15 minutes.

Skin the fillets and remove the little bones - see instructions on page 39.

Spread each fillet with a little mayonnaise and season lightly. Then roll up. It is a personal preference whether you roll up from the narrow end or the wide end. (If necessary, hold in position with a wooden cocktail stick .) Place on a lightly greased ovenproof dish, spread a little more mayonnaise on the top of each 'roll'. Bake in a moderately hot oven until cooked through. (Remove cocktail sticks.)

Decorate with a little chopped parsley and a wedge of lemon.

How Cajun got its name !

In 1755 British soldiers drove a colony of French settlers out of Acadia in Nova Scotia. This group of dispossessed French, settled in the swamplands of Louisiana (which no one else wanted!) and became known as the Acadians. The pronunciation of this name evolved over the years into Cajuns. Many other ethnic influences (African, Spanish, Caribbean etc.) are to be found in Cajun cooking, but the French influence is an important one. The staple ingredients of Cajun cooking were whatever they could hunt, catch, or grow, such as shrimp, alligators, oysters, sweet potato, okra and so on. The main spices are black pepper, cayenne pepper and paprika.

Seafood Jambalaya

This is my version of a typical Cajun dish. Rice is traditionally included in it but I prefer to cook it separately for speed.

This dish is cooked in a frying pan on top of the cooker - though if numbers are too large to fit, it can be finished off in the oven.

1 onion, chopped
1 tablespoon oil
2 cloves garlic, chopped or crushed
1 green pepper, deseeded and chopped
2 stalks celery, chopped (about 50g/2oz)
1 tin chopped tomatoes
Salt and freshly ground pepper
Quarter teaspoon cayenne pepper
Half teaspoon mixed herbs
Juice half lemon
4 teaspoons chopped fresh parsley
1 tin (200g) prawns, drained
4 - 5 pieces of salmon fillet (110g/4oz each)
Cajun seasoning (optional)

Note: Do not remove the skin from the salmon as this holds the fish together during cooking and makes it easier to lift out afterwards.

Fry the onion in the oil until soft, adding in the garlic as it fries. Add the pepper and celery and stir in the tinned tomatoes. Season with salt, pepper, cayenne pepper, herbs, lemon juice and half the parsley.

Simmer gently to allow some of the juices of the pan to evaporate (don't overdo it though, as the sauce should be somewhat runny rather than a thick purée)

Add the prawns to the pan. Then place the salmon pieces down into the vegetable mix, but allowing most of the top surface to remain visible. Season the top of the fish with Cajun seasoning or a sprinkling of salt and pepper and a tiny pinch of cayenne.

Cover the pan (use foil if no lid is available) and simmer gently for about 10 minutes or until the fish is cooked. This you can judge by separating the flesh in the thickest part and checking that it has turned the same colour the whole way through.

Serve sprinkled with the remaining parsley, accompanied with rice, pasta or crusty bread.

Salmon and Spinach Loaf

(Serves 6)

Tasty, simple and economical (uses tinned salmon), the little bit of spinach is optional, but it gives the loaf a nice speckled look .

1 onion, chopped
2 cloves garlic, chopped
2 - 3 tablespoons oil
175g (6oz) mushrooms, chopped
2 x 200g tins of salmon
150g (5oz) breadcrumbs, (preferably wholemeal)
110g (4oz) frozen spinach leaf, thawed
2 large eggs
2 generous tablespoons mayonnaise
Juice half lemon
Salt and freshly ground black pepper
Generous pinches of mixed herbs
Pinches of nutmeg

Tin: Loaf tin 23cm x 12.5cm x 7.5cm deep (9" x 5" x 3"). Line the base with baking parchment or foil, to facilitate turning out the loaf after cooking.

Preheat Oven: 185°C, 360°F Gas 4½ - in other words - just a little hotter than moderate.

Cooking Time: About 50 - 60 minutes.

Fry the onion and garlic in the oil until soft. Then add in the mushrooms and fry until they too are soft and tasty. Transfer the contents of the pan into a mixing bowl. Drain the juice from the tins of salmon (save it for the Lemon and Parsley Sauce) and put the fish into the mixing bowl along with the breadcrumbs. Into a separate bowl, put the spinach, eggs, mayonnaise and lemon juice and whisk together OR buzz them in a food processor. The spinach will get chopped up in the process. Add this liquid mixture to the salmon mixture. Season and flavour with the herbs and nutmeg. Mix everything together well.

Pour the mixture into the prepared tin, smoothing it out. Cover the tin tightly with oiled foil and bake in the oven . Remove the foil for the last 10 - 15 minutes to allow the top get lightly browned. Turn out and serve with the Lemon and Parsley Sauce (see opposite page).

Tuna and Mushroom Loaf

A variation on the above loaf - use tuna instead of salmon (choosing tuna in brine rather than oil). Omit the spinach, instead use **110g (4oz) extra mushrooms**.

Serve with the Lemon and Parsley Sauce (see opposite page) - adding the brine from the tin of tuna.

Lemon and Parsley Sauce

Made in a jiffy!

Juices from the two tins of salmon (see note)
Enough milk to bring the juices to 275ml (half pt)
25g (1oz) <u>each</u> of margarine and flour
2 tablespoons chopped fresh parsley
2 tablespoons fresh lemon juice
Salt and freshly ground black pepper
Pinches of nutmeg
1 slice onion

Note: This sauce can be made with any juices from cooked fish. If no juices available, simply use 275ml (half pt) of milk.

Put all the ingredients into a saucepan. Use a whisk to stir briskly while cooking over a gentle heat until everything melts and blends together. Then raise the heat and bring to the boil to thicken, stirring all the time. Lift out and discard the slice of onion.

We are constantly being recommended to eat oily fish for our hearts sake. Research on Eskimos, who eat a diet almost entirely of fish, show they suffer from less heart attacks. Also if they cut themselves, they bleed copiously - proof that their blood doesn't clot easily! All fats are made up of different fatty acids, certain beneficial fatty acids are found in greater quantity in oily fish.

Speedy Tuna Fish and Tomato Tart (Serves 4 - 5)

A piece of puff pastry, laid out flat, is covered with tomatoes and tuna, leaving a narrow margin all around the edge. This puffs up when baked and looks like a tart. You can even buy ready rolled puff pastry !

Ready-rolled pastry (approx. 23cm x 28cm/9" x 11")
OR half packet of frozen puff pastry
1 onion, chopped
2 tablespoons oil
1 - 2 cloves garlic, crushed
110g (4oz) mushrooms, chopped
1 tin (200g) of tuna fish, drained
75g (3oz) breadcrumbs (white or wholemeal)
Salt and freshly ground black pepper
A little finely grated lemon rind
A few pinches of oregano OR mixed herbs
1 tablespoon chopped fresh parsley
1 - 2 tablespoons mayonnaise (optional)
About 4 tomatoes, sliced
50g (2oz) grated cheese

Tin: Flat Baking tin approx. 23cm x 33cm (9" x 13"), lightly greased

Preheat Oven: Hot oven, 200°C, 400°F gas 6

Cooking Time: About 25 minutes.

Unroll the piece of ready rolled puff pastry and cut to the size of the tin (or roll out the puff pastry into a similar rectangular or square shape). Place on the prepared tin.

Fry the onion in the oil until soft, adding in the garlic as it fries. Add in the chopped mushrooms and fry for a few minutes to soften them. Stir in the tuna fish and the breadcrumbs. Season with salt and pepper. Flavour with the grated lemon rind, the oregano and chopped parsley. Finally, stir in the mayonnaise. Spread this mixture over the pastry leaving a narrow margin all around the edge (about 3cm/1½" wide). Lay the sliced tomatoes in a layer over the top, scattering with the grated cheese.

Bake until the pastry is well cooked. Serve hot.

Chicken and Turkey

Roast Chicken Layered Loaf

(Serves 5 - 6)

This recipe could be described as a simplified version of a boned stuffed roast chicken. I 'invented' it to solve the family problem of everyone wanting the breast and discovered that this recipe makes a chicken into a special dish. Equally good served hot or cold! It is quite an easy task to prepare the chicken, but you can ask your butcher to do it for you if you give him the directions (see below).

1 chicken, medium/ large
1 onion, chopped
2 tablespoons oil
1 - 2 cloves garlic
150g (5oz) mushrooms, finely chopped
50g (2oz) wholemeal breadcrumbs
1 tablespoon chopped fresh parsley
Salt and freshly ground black pepper
Quarter or half teaspoon herbes de Provence
1 - 2 tablespoons soy sauce
1 large egg

Tin: Loaf tin (23cm x 12.5cm x 7.5cm deep/9' x 5" x 3" deep), greased.

Preheat Oven: 190°C, 375°F, Gas 5.

Cooking Time: After about 30 minutes reduce to 180°C, 350°F, Gas 4 and cook a further 40 - 60 minutes.

Directions to prepare chicken: Cut off the legs and wings. Remove flesh off the carcass **all in one piece,** with as much as possible of the skin still attached (the flesh will naturally include the two breasts). To do this, start at the back and cut the skin from neck to tail. Then simply start at one side of this slit and pare away the flesh from the bone, all the way round the carcass until you come right round to the back again, on the other side . The meat comes away quite easily, the only place to watch is at the high breast bone because there is very little flesh there. The chicken meat (breasts included) can now be laid out flat in one piece. It will look ragged and a bit untidy, but the more skin attached the better.

Prepare the loaf: Place the prepared chicken flesh (with the breasts included), skin side downwards, into the greased tin, allowing the extra flesh/skin to run up the sides. If necessary rearrange some of the breast flesh to make a fairly even layer of breast meat over the base of the tin.

Cut the flesh off the legs, wings and any that remains on the carcass. Remove the skin. (The skin and bones can be used to make a stock for soup.) Mince (or finely chop) the meat. (I do it in the food processor for a few seconds.) Put it into a bowl.

Fry the onion in the oil, adding in the garlic and mushrooms, until soft and tasty. Add to the minced chicken, with the breadcrumbs and parsley. Season with the salt, pepper, herbs and soy sauce. Add the egg and mix well.

Put this mixture into the chicken lined tin and smooth evenly out. Fold any flaps of the skin over the top. Cover the tin loosely with a piece of foil. Bake in the oven (removing the foil for the last half hour) until nicely cooked.

Pour off the juices (use in gravy) and gently turn out the 'loaf' onto an ovenproof plate. The skin of the chicken will probably look like it has been boiled ! To crisp it nicely return the loaf, on the plate, to a hot oven (200°C, 400°F, Gas 6) for about 10 - 20 minutes, until the skin turns a lovely golden brown just like a roast chicken.

Allow to stand for about 10 minutes before slicing and use a sharp knife to prevent breaking up the slices.

Serving note: Some juices from the chicken loaf will come onto the plate and will dry up during the browning. While this is okay for family, it may not look the greatest when serving guests! To camouflage this and add colour to the finished dish, I suggest placing an over lapping row of sliced tomatoes, alternating with sliced courgettes, all around the loaf, brush with the poured off juices and season with salt and pepper. They will cook lightly while the chicken loaf browns.

Chicken and Bacon Bites

Bite-size chunks of chicken breast can be used instead of the cod in the recipe for Cod and Bacon Bites (page 29). Use **about 2 - 3 chicken breasts.** These will take a little longer to cook.

If Henry IV of France could take a leap in time from the 1590s to the 1990s, he would be amazed that one of his wishes had more than come true. This benevolent monarch, after tasting the delicious Poulet au Pot, that classic chicken recipe, wished to create an economy, where each of his subjects could afford to enjoy chicken on a Sunday. Chicken has since evolved from a luxury meal into an easily accessible meat.

Not surprisingly, chicken is common to all cuisines, due to it's versatility and the vast range of ingredients with which it will blend. (Furthermore, the consumption of chicken is encouraged by the medical profession, because of its low saturated fat content.) Sold in all shapes and sizes from the whole chicken, to the wide range of chicken portions, in various stages of preparation, including the frozen cooked chicken dishes ready to eat as soon as you hear the 'ping' of the microwave.

Chicken with a Secret Heart

Each boneless chicken breast fillet has a little 'pocket' slit in it, which is filled with a tasty stuffing. A back rasher is wrapped around the outside and it is fried gently until cooked through. A little cream and a dash of dry sherry added to the pan make a tasty, instant sauce . Providing the stuffing is quite cold, these can be assembled hours in advance and cooked before serving.

For 2 servings:
The ingredients can be increased as required, but don't increase the cream and sherry at quite the same rate!
2 back rashers
2 good sized boneless chicken breast fillets
75ml (3fl.oz) fresh cream
2 - 3 teaspoons dry /medium dry sherry
A little oil for frying

Stuffing:
Half small onion
1 very small clove garlic
1 tablespoon olive oil
50g (2oz) mushrooms
1 small stick celery
1 tablespoon wholemeal breadcrumbs
Salt and freshly ground black pepper
Pinch mixed herbs
2 teaspoons chopped fresh parsley
1 tablespoon stock or orange juice (optional)

Rinse the rashers in a little cold water to remove a little of the saltiness and pat them dry. Cut a slit right into the chicken breast to make a 'pocket'. If there is a flap (mini-fillet) of flesh at the back of the chicken breast you can leave it or remove it (using it another time).

Make the stuffing: It is important to chop everything very finely. First fry the chopped onion and garlic in the oil until soft, then add in the finely chopped mushrooms and celery, and fry until soft. Transfer contents of the pan to a bowl. Then add the breadcrumbs, salt, pepper, mixed herbs, parsley and orange juice and mix well together.

Assemble and cook: Fill the 'pockets' in the chicken with the stuffing.

Wrap a rasher round the centre of each stuffed breast folding the ends neatly in underneath. Fry in a little oil, placing the underside down onto the pan first as this 'sets' the rasher in position. When golden turn over and brown the top side. Continue frying over a gentle heat , turning occasionally. Cover the pan loosely with foil (keeps heat in) until the chicken is cooked through. This will take at least 20 minutes. Lift-out chicken and pour a little fresh cream and a dash of sherry into the juices in the pan and season lightly. Cook briskly for a few minutes and serve on the chicken.

Arroz Con Pollo (Spanish-Style Chicken)

(Serves 4 - 6)

A tasty Spanish recipe with chicken, rice and vegetables all cooked in one pot. It cooks fairly quickly. The rice is coloured yellow, traditionally with saffron threads, but I use turmeric since it is easier on my pocket ! The finished dish looks most colourful as the yellow rice is dappled with the bright red of the peppers and sharp green of the peas.

1 medium chicken, divided into 6 portions
2 tablespoons oil
1 onion, chopped
2 cloves garlic, crushed
1 large red pepper, deseeded and chopped
225g (8oz) fresh tomatoes, chopped
Salt and freshly ground black pepper
Quarter teaspoon cayenne pepper
1 teaspoon paprika
225g (8oz) long grained rice
570ml (1 pt) chicken stock
1 glass dry sherry
1 teaspoon turmeric
110g (4oz) frozen peas, thawed

Preheat Oven: 180°C, 350°F, Gas 4.

Cooking Time: About 1 hour.

Fry the chicken portions in the oil to brown them and transfer to a wide-based casserole. Fry the chopped onion and garlic and when soft add in the chopped pepper and chopped tomatoes. Season well and add the cayenne pepper and paprika. Add the rice and pour in the stock, sherry and turmeric. Stir and pour the whole lot into the casserole with the chicken. Cover with a lid and cook in the oven for about 40 minutes. Then add the peas and continue to cook for another 20 minutes or more until well cooked.

French Casserole (Cassoulet) – Irish Style (Serves 6)

A delicious combination of ingredients.

Cassoulet is a traditional dish from the south-west area of France. Like all traditional recipes it varies a lot. The basic ingredients include a variety of meats cooked with beans - haricot beans. To give it an Irish variation, I use chicken and ham (or bacon) and instead of the beans I use marrowfat peas. To prevent the marrowfat peas getting very mushy, they are added in approximately halfway through the cooking.

250g (9oz) marrowfat peas
700g (1½ lb) lean ham or bacon, cut in generous chunks
6 chicken portions (700g/1½ lb)
A little oil for frying
2 onions, cut in quarters
1 - 2 cloves garlic
2 - 3 sticks celery, chopped
275g (10oz) carrots, sliced
About 700ml (1¼ pt) chicken stock
Salt and freshly ground black pepper
Mixed herbs, (use dried and/or fresh herbs)
2 whole cloves, apple tart kind
3 heaped teaspoons cornflour (optional)

To serve: chopped fresh parsley

Note: If cooking in advance, prepare only steps 1 and 2. Leave step 3 until about 40 minutes before serving.

Step 1: Steep the marrowfat peas overnight, by covering them well with hot water. Put the chunks of ham (or bacon) into another bowl of cold water and leave to steep overnight.

Step 2: Next day drain the water off both the peas and the ham. Put the ham into a large saucepan.

Fry the chicken portions until golden brown, put into the saucepan with the ham. Lightly fry the onions and garlic and add to the meats. Add in the celery, carrots, stock, seasoning, herbs and cloves. The amount of stock may seem small but the juices come from the meat during cooking. Bring to the boil and simmer gently with a lid on, for about 45 minutes until the meat is tender.

Step 3: Add in the marrowfat peas and bring the contents of the saucepan to the boil again and then simmer gently for about another half hour or more until the peas are cooked and everything is deliciously tender. (If you wish to thicken the juices, add the cornflour, blended with a little water into the saucepan, stir and bring to the boil .) Serve scattered generously with fresh parsley.

Picture opposite: Fillets of Trout with Pesto and Prawns

Poulet au Pot

(Serves 5 - 6)

Traditionally cooked in plenty of water, which made a tasty broth, the flavour-some boiling fowl required is no longer readily available. The following is my adaptation of the recipe, using very little liquid and some bacon with the vegetables adding greater flavour to the modern roasting chicken. This dish can be left to cook slowly and deliciously in the oven while you do something else.

Medium/ large roasting chicken
2 tablespoons olive oil
1 large onion, chopped
2 - 3 cloves garlic, chopped
4 - 5 rashers
1 large carrot, chopped
2 sticks celery, chopped
2 bay leaves
Sprig of parsley
Half teaspoon herbes de Provence
Salt and freshly ground black pepper
1 glass of white wine
425ml (three quarters pt) tasty chicken stock
(OR if necessary use water and 1 chicken stock cube)
1 - 2 heaped teaspoons cornflour (optional)

To serve: Chopped fresh parsley

Preheat Oven: 180°C, 350°F, Gas 4.

Cooking Time: About 1½ hours.

Fry the chicken all over in the oil as best you can, to brown the outside and put to one side. Fry the onions and garlic and put into a casserole. Then fry the rashers, and put one rasher on the breast of the chicken and the rest into the casserole. Add the carrot and celery, the herbs and seasoning into the casserole and pour in the wine and stock. (Using boiling stock slightly speeds up the cooking time.) Sit the chicken in on top of everything. Cover the casserole with a lid and put into the centre of the oven. Cook until the chicken is very tender. (If cooked at a lower temperature 150°C, 300°F, Gas 2, it will take twice as long to cook.)

The juices can be thickened as follows, blend the cornflour with a little drop of cold water. Strain the juices into the chicken and put into a saucepan with the blended cornflour and bring to the boil. Pour back over the chicken. Serve with the vegetables and scatter with the parsley.

Picture opposite: Banoffi Pie

Overleaf Left: Scalloped Ham (or Bacon) and Potatoes

Overleaf Right: Chicken with a Secret Heart

Russian Chicken Salad

There was a time when Russian salad was a very popular salad in Ireland. This salad has the distinction that the vegetables used are cooked, except for the spring onions! Beetroot was an essential ingredient. This is a nice variation that includes cooked chicken. The salad is laid on an large oval serving plate and looks very well indeed.

110g (4oz) peas, cooked
110g (4oz) carrots, cooked and diced
1 - 2 gherkins or pickles, chopped
Small bunch spring onions (scallions), washed and chopped
Salt and freshly ground black pepper
French dressing (see page 100)
About 450g (1 lb) small potatoes, steamed or boiled in their skins
175g (6oz) cooked chicken, cut in narrow strips
3 hard boiled eggs, cut into quarters - down the length
6 cherry tomatoes, halved
Half jar sliced beetroot, drained
1 tablespoon chopped fresh parsley

To serve: mayonnaise or salad dressing.

In a bowl, mix together the peas and carrots, also the gherkin and spring onions. Season with salt and pepper and moisten with some of the dressing. Pile this mixture into the centre of an oval plate.

Peel and cut the potatoes in quarters or sixths, depending on size and arrange them all around the central pile of vegetables in such a way that the end of each 'wedge' is pointing outwards - almost like the petals on a daisy. Season with salt and freshly ground black pepper.

Next arrange the chicken strips on top of the potatoes, all pointing outwards also. Place the eggs (pointing in the same way as the potatoes) around the central pile of peas and carrots. Scatter the cherry tomatoes on top of the central pile of vegetables. Finally, arrange the slices of beetroot (halving them if they are too big) side-by-side all around the edge of the plate, tucking them in a little under the points of the potatoes. Dribble more dressing over the top of everything and scatter with the chopped parsley. Serve with mayonnaise or salad dressing.

Bengal Salad

(Serves 4)

A shop bought, ready-roasted chicken can be transformed into a home-made dish in this recipe. Naturally if you have your own cooked chicken all the better!

A little curry powder and chutney added to the mayonnaise gives an Indian touch to this tasty chicken salad.

Salad:
350g (12oz) cooked chicken, chopped
1 banana, chopped
1 eating apple, chopped
Half medium cucumber, chopped
4 - 6 scallions, chopped
3 - 4 tablespoons chopped pineapple
1 - 2 sticks celery, chopped

Dressing:
4 tablespoons mayonnaise
1 teaspoon curry paste
Juice half orange
1 teaspoon finely grated orange rind
2 - 3 teaspoons mango chutney
1 teaspoon grated root ginger (optional)

To serve:
Shredded lettuce or 4 cooked poppadums

Mix all the salad ingredients together in a bowl. In a separate container whisk together the dressing ingredients and then pour them over the salad. Toss together and leave to stand in a cool place for about one hour before serving.

Serve on leaves of lettuce or on cooked poppadums, and accompany with crusty bread.

Chicken with Tomatoes and Ginger

(Serves 4 - 5)

Use the recipe for Salmon with Tomatoes and Ginger (page 31) substituting the salmon with 4 - 5 medium chicken breasts. Lightly brown the outside of the breasts before putting into the hot ovenproof dish. The cooking time will be approximately 30 minutes.

Stuffing Topped Turkey Breast Steaks

(Serves about 4 - 5)

The turkey breast steaks are placed flat on a greased tin or ovenproof dish, topped with a simple but tasty stuffing and baked in the oven. As well as flavour the stuffing also makes the steaks more substantial.

450 - 550g (1 - 1¼ lb) turkey breast steaks
2 - 3 tablespoons water (for the tin)

Stuffing:
1 onion, chopped
2 tablespoons oil
1 clove garlic, crushed
2 sticks celery, chopped finely
1 small - medium cooking apple, chopped finely
75g (3oz) breadcrumbs, preferably wholemeal
A few pinches oregano (or mixed herbs)
1 tablespoon chopped fresh parsley
1 teaspoon finely grated orange rind
Half teaspoon sugar
Juice 1 orange
2 - 3 tablespoons water
Quarter chicken stock cube
Salt and freshly ground black pepper

Preheat Oven: Moderately hot oven (190°C, 375°F, Gas 5).

Cooking Time: About 30 - 40 minutes.

Lay the turkey breast steaks flat on a greased ovenproof dish or tin. If some of the pieces are too small, lay two right beside each other, as if one.

To make the stuffing, fry the onion in the oil until soft, adding the garlic as it cooks. Next add in the celery, apple and breadcrumbs. Flavour with the herbs, parsley, orange rind and sugar. Mix the orange juice with the water and mash the stock cube through, then add this liquid to the stuffing. Season with the pepper. Salt may not be necessary because of the stock cube - but taste and see !

Pile this tasty stuffing on top of the turkey breasts, pressing down to secure in place. Spoon a little water into the dish and cover well with foil. Bake until cooked through.

For the last 10 minutes of cooking, remove the foil cover (and pour off any juices). Cook until the stuffing is crisp.

Serve with gravy.

Turkey, Broccoli and Orange Stir-Fry (Serves 4)

The turkey, broccoli and orange combination are excellent in this speedy stir-fry.

450g (1 lb) turkey breast steaks
450g (1 lb) broccoli, washed and cut in florets
1 orange
1 - 2 tablespoons oil
1 small onion, chopped thinly
2 sticks celery, sliced thinly

Sauce:
1 heaped teaspoon cornflour
Juice 1 orange
Enough water to make up 150ml (quarter pt)
2 tablespoons soy sauce
1 teaspoon brown (or white) sugar
Freshly ground black pepper

Prepare the turkey by cutting it into narrow fingers (cut across the grain).

Cook the broccoli in boiling salted water (or steam) for about 10 minutes until almost tender. Drain well.

Peel the orange with a sharp knife, removing all the pith so just the flesh shows. Carefully cut out each segment of orange from between the membranes (thin inner skin). Make up the stir-fry sauce by mixing all the sauce ingredients together.

Using a wok or a wide saucepan, fry the turkey fingers (in two lots) in the oil. When they are lightly golden and cooked through, lift out. Next fry the onion and celery, until soft. Add the broccoli and cook lightly for a minute or two. Put the cooked turkey pieces back in and stir in the prepared sauce. Cook everything together, tossing and stirring, while bringing to the boil to thicken . Add in the orange segments. Heat through.

Serve immediately with boiled rice or Chinese noodles.

Shopping at the last minute and whizzing by the chilled meat cabinet, I often pick up a packet of turkey breast steaks, thinking that they will cook quickly without leaving too much of a hole in my pocket! However, separated from its natural skin and bone, the meat is stripped of a lot of its flavour. So, in order to cook successfully, it needs added flavour - as in these tasty recipes.

Chicken with Lemon and Olives (Serves 4 - 6)

The Greek style ingredients of lemon and olives, give an unusual sharp tangy flavour to the chicken which makes a nice change. If prepared in advance and reheated the flavours will 'mellow' together even more.

1 small/ medium chicken divided into 4 - 6 portions
2 tablespoons olive oil
1 onion, chopped
2 cloves garlic, chopped
1 lemon, cut in narrow wedges
Salt and freshly ground black pepper
Half teaspoon herbes de Provence
275ml (half pt) tasty chicken stock (if necessary use 1 stock cube)
50g (2oz) green olives, stones removed
1 heaped teaspoon cornflour

Preheat Oven: 180°C, 350°F, Gas 4

Cooking Time: About 1 hour

Fry the chicken portions in the oil to brown them and transfer to a casserole. Fry the onion and garlic and put with the chicken. Half squeeze the lemon wedges over the chicken and then place the half-squeezed wedges on top of the chicken. Add the seasonings and herbs and pour in the stock. Cover and cook in the oven until tender. Add the olives for the last 15 minutes of cooking. If liked pour off the juices and thicken by boiling with the cornflour (blended with a little water). Pour back over the chicken.

Turkey Olives

Use the recipe for the Beef Olives (page 66). Substitute **6 - 8 slices of turkey breast** for the beef and use **chicken stock** instead of beef stock. The cooking time will be about three quarters - 1 hour.

Meat

Butterflied Leg of Lamb

(Serves 1 person for every 175g(6oz) lean meat)

Butterflied leg of lamb is delicious and a dream to carve! The recipe comes to us from America. The bone is cut out from the centre of a leg of lamb and instead of rolling the flesh up again, it is left lying flat. Seemingly, this shape looks like a butterfly! Though to me it looks more like a model of small mountains, because of the uneven lumps of lean flesh!

The butcher will 'butterfly' the joint for you. Since removing the bone from any joint always removes some of the flavour, a tasty marinade spooned over the meat is important.

The meat is cooked in the oven, though the final browning can be done on the barbecue.

1 leg of lamb, prepared in butterfly shape

Marinade:
4 tablespoons oil (preferably olive oil)
2 tablespoons wine vinegar
1 tablespoon lemon juice
1 teaspoon grated lemon rind
Half teaspoon French mustard
2 - 4 cloves garlic, crushed
Quarter teaspoon herbes de Provence
Quarter teaspoon dried rosemary (see note)
Salt and freshly ground black pepper

Note: ideally use a few sprigs of fresh rosemary, putting a few bits into the marinade and scattering the rest over the meat itself.

Tin: If your roasting tin is not wide enough for the butterflied leg to lie flat, simply use a baking tin.

Preheat Oven: 180°C, 350°F, Gas 4.

Cooking Time: Approximately 45 minutes to serve pink, leave in longer if you want it well-done. After roasting, leave meat to stand and relax for about 20 minutes. (Cover with foil to keep heat in.)

Trim off excess fat. Place the lamb out flat (skin side underneath) on a baking or roasting tray. If any of the "lumps" of lean meat on the lamb seem larger than the rest, you can slit them with a knife. This ensures that the meat cooks evenly, also it allows the flavour of the marinade to penetrate more.

Mix together the marinade ingredients and spoon all over the lamb. Cover and leave in the fridge (or a cool place) for a few hours, ideally overnight. Remove from the fridge at least an hour before cooking so that it comes to room temperature. Roast the joint uncovered until done the way you like it. Remember that after cooking, while the roast 'relaxes' before carving, it will continue to cook in it's own heat.

You can test for 'doneness' by piercing the thickest part with a skewer and catching the juices in a spoon. If they are pink, the lamb will also be pink. If you'd prefer the meat well done continue cooking until the juices are clear or lightly golden.

To finish on barbecue: If preferred, the joint can get the final browning on the barbecue for the last 20 minutes or so. Cooking time on a barbecue can vary enormously. A barbecue with a lid will cook much more quickly because the heat is trapped inside.

Lamb Kebabs

Kebabs require tender meat that will cook quickly and this means using the more expensive cuts. Because I like my meat well cooked I usually don't include vegetables on the skewers as they will only scorch while the meat cooks.

700g (1½ lb) of lean lamb (leg), cut in cubes
Marinade as for the Butterflied Leg of lamb (opposite page)

If using bamboo skewers, steep them in cold water for about 30 minutes so they won't burn easily.

Put the lamb into the marinade for about 3 - 4 hours. Cover and stir occasionally. Thread the meat onto the skewers and grill or barbecue until cooked to your satisfaction.

Beef Olives (Paupiettes of Beef)

(Serves 5 - 6)

Ideal for a special occasion. Improves with reheating, so make the day before.

Thin raw slices of beef are stuffed and rolled, and then cooked in a casserole with some vegetables and stock. The butcher will cut the meat thinly for you and will batten each piece between two pieces of baking parchment or plastic to make them nice and thin.

700 - 900g (1½ - 2 lb) lean beef (topside or silverside) cut into 6 - 8 thin slices of lean round steak, each weighing about 110g/4oz and flattened thin

Stuffing:
1 small onion, chopped
1 - 2 cloves garlic, crushed
2 - 3 tablespoons olive oil
175g (6oz) mushrooms, chopped
175g (6oz) rashers
Salt and freshly ground black pepper
Generous pinches of mixed herbs
A few pinches nutmeg
Wooden cocktail sticks or fine string
2-3 tablespoons of oil for frying

Sauce:
1 large onion, chopped
2 cloves garlic, chopped
50g (2oz) mushrooms, sliced
About 1 tablespoon oil
1 carrot, diced.
2 sticks celery, chopped
1 heaped teaspoon tomato purée
About 425ml (three quarters pt) beef stock
Salt and freshly ground black pepper
Mixed herbs

To serve: Chopped fresh parsley

Make up the stuffing: Fry the onion and garlic together in 2 tablespoons of the oil. Add the mushrooms and fry until they soften, then lift out everything with a perforated spoon. Buzz this mixture in a food processor to chop finely - almost like breadcrumbs. Put into bowl. Next fry the rashers. When cooked drain them on a paper towel. Buzz them in a food processor, to chop them very finely. Put into the bowl with the onions and mushrooms. Add the rest of the stuffing ingredients and mix together.

Divide the stuffing mixture between the pieces of meat, spread out and roll them up (like little Swiss rolls). Hold in position with cocktail sticks, or tie with fine string. (If using cocktail sticks - ensure that they are all sticking into the beef olives (beef rolls) in the same direction otherwise it will be impossible to fry them if the sticks are popping out in all directions.)

Fry the beef olives to brown the outside, lift out and put to one side.

To prepare the sauce: Fry the onion, garlic and mushrooms in the oil and transfer to a saucepan or casserole adding the remaining vegetables. Sit the beef olives on top. Mix the tomato purée into the stock and pour over the meat. Season with salt and freshly ground black pepper and add the mixed herbs. If liked add half a glass of wine. Cover the saucepan with a lid, bring to the boil and simmer gently for about 1½ hours, or longer, until tender.

If preferred, cook in a casserole in a moderately slow oven (180°C, 350°F, Gas 4) for about 2 hours until tender (reduce heat if necessary).

To serve: Drain off the juices and remove any fat from the surface (dab lightly with a paper towel). Blend 2 heaped teaspoons cornflour with a little cold water and add to the juices. Bring to the boil to thicken and then add back to the meat and vegetables. Serve, sprinkled with chopped parsley.

It is an interesting nutritional fact that vitamin C (ascorbic acid) helps the body absorb iron from the food we eat - especially from grains. Meat, itself a good source of iron, also helps the absorption of iron from other foods. Vitamin C is available not only in oranges, but in most fresh fruits and vegetables.

Non-meat sources of iron include shellfish and oily fish, eggs, whole grains, nuts, dried fruits, treacle and cocoa.

Classic Beef Casserole (Serves 5 - 6)

This is based on the famous French recipe Bœuf Bourguignonne. This recipe lifts the 'casserole' into the realm of haute cuisine! It is special enough for any party or if you wish to really spoil your family. The combination of ingredients is basically very simple with the red wine making the difference.

Another important point is the preliminary browning of the meat and onions as this enhances the flavour of the finished dish. I prefer to do this on a pan, transferring the food to a saucepan or casserole. As with most casseroles, it improves if left over night and reheated.

700 - 900g (1½ - 2 lb) stewing beef (see note)
3 - 4 tablespoons oil, to brown meat
4 - 5 streaky rashers (preferably smoked)
2 medium onions, chopped
2 - 3 cloves garlic, chopped
175g (6oz) mushrooms, quartered
2 sticks celery, chopped
425ml (three-quarters pt) beef stock (if necessary use a cube)
275ml (half pt) red wine
2 tablespoons tomato purée
Salt and freshly ground black pepper
Mixed herbs
To finish:
175g (6oz) shallots or button onions, peeled
175g (6oz) button mushrooms
2 - 3 tablespoons oil
1 teaspoon sugar

Note: I frequently use a combination of round and rib steaks. The round is nice and lean, but the rib has a better flavour.

Cut the beef into chunks, discarding any fat or membrane. Brown the meat (in three lots) in some of the oil. Transfer to the saucepan or casserole. Brown the rashers and add them to the meat. Wipe out the pan, put in the remaining oil and fry the onions, garlic and mushrooms, when soft put with the meat.

Add the celery, stock, wine, tomato purée, the seasoning and herbs. If using a saucepan, bring to the boil, then turn heat right down to barely simmering and cook, covered, until tender. It will take at least 1½ hours.

If preferred, cook in a casserole, in the oven preheated to 150°C, 300°F, Gas 2, and cook for 3 hours until tender.

Half an hour before the end of the cooking time fry the shallots and the button mushrooms until they are a nice golden brown colour. As they fry, sprinkle the sugar over them. Drain on absorbent paper towels and add to the casserole.

Roast Beef

The most important factor to take into consideration, when buying a joint of beef is to ensure that it has been well hung. If it isn't, the meat will be tough. Ordinary roasting will not tenderise tough meat, so buy from a reliable butcher.

The nicest way to cook roast beef is on the bone. The bone imparts flavour and is a good conductor of heat, it also keeps the meat together better, making it simpler to carve. Despite the modern guidelines towards leaner meat, a better roast is achieved with a certain amount of fat present, because it gives flavour and keeps the joint moist. Little flecks of fat ("marbling") should be visible through the lean meat, as well as some outside fat. Most of the fat either melts off during cooking or can be cut away after cooking. Ideally have a rack of some kind in your roasting tin, so that the meat is not sitting in the melted fat.

The best joints to choose are a **Rib Roast** (ask for the two or three ribs nearest to the sirloin) or **Sirloin Roast (T-bone included)**. Ideally a joint of beef should be **at least 2 - 2.5kg (4 - 5 lb)** in weight, smaller joints do not roast as successfully. Allow about 350g (12oz) meat on the bone, per serving. Unless already done, ask the butcher to cut the ribs short and remove the chine bone for easy carving.

Preheat Oven: 200°C, 400°F, Gas 6.

Cooking Time: Roast the joint for 15 minutes at the high temperature, then reduce the temperature to 180°C, 350°F, Gas 4 and continue roasting for the following times:

For rare beef - allowing about 15 minutes roasting for every 450g (1 lb) of meat being cooked.

For medium-done - allow same time as for rare beef **plus** an extra 20 minutes.

For well-done - allow the same time as for the rare beef **plus** an extra 30 minutes.

I recommend using a meat thermometer as it takes a lot of the guess work out of the cooking. Stick the thermometer into the thickest part of the meat, but don't touch the bone as this will get very hot. The internal reading for rare is 60°C, medium 70°C and 80°C for well done.

About 2 hours before roasting, remove the meat from the fridge and leave to stand in the kitchen to come to room temperature. Brush the lean surface of the meat with **a little oil.** Sit the roast on the tin with the fat side uppermost (see note). Rub **some mustard (or curry powder), salt and freshly ground black pepper** into the fat. Roast as directed. Baste occasionally with the juices.

After roasting, leave the meat to sit at the side of the cooker for about 30 minutes to 'rest', before carving. I usually cover with foil, with a tea-towel on top to keep in the heat.

Strain the fat off the roasting juices and add the juices to your gravy.

Spiced Beef

Traditionally served at Christmas time in Ireland, it is becoming increasingly popular to serve at any time! Good on crackers served as 'finger food' or on a cold buffet table. Long slow cooking is the best for spiced beef. Ideally, it should be cooked in a fairly snugly-fitting saucepan, as too much liquid dilutes the flavour - (but ensure that there is enough liquid to last for the long slow cooking). A nice heavy saucepan with a good fitting lid is a great help. If the joint I am cooking only fits into one of my bigger saucepans, then I'll add only enough liquid to half cover the meat, turning it over a couple of times during cooking so that both sides cook the same.

Joint of spiced beef
Water
1 beef stock cube
1 onion, quartered
1 stick celery, chopped
Half cooking apple
Generous pinches of nutmeg
A few whole cloves
1 glass sherry
50g (2oz) brown sugar

Put the beef into a saucepan and add enough water to just barely cover. Add in all the other ingredients. Bring to the boil and then simmer gently until the meat is tender. This will take about three-quarters hour for every 450g (1 lb) of meat being cooked, with an extra three-quarters hour at the end.

Traditionally served cold but it can also be served hot. Allow to cool in the cooking water.

Accompany with chutney.

Peppered Steaks   (Serves 2)

A quick, tasty dinner for two or more, multiply the ingredients accordingly.

2 tender steaks (sirloin or fillet)
1 tablespoon black peppercorns
25g (1oz) butter
1 tablespoon olive oil
1 tablespoon brandy or whiskey
75ml (3fl.oz) fresh cream
Salt, if necessary

Trim any excess fat off the meat. Crush the peppercorns coarsely (on a wooden board using a rolling pin). Press the peppercorns into the surface of the meat. Heat the butter and oil in a heavy-based frying pan, cook the steaks over a high heat for 2 minutes, turning them once. This is to seal in the juices. Lower the heat and cook until done as required. For rare steak allow about 5 minutes, 8-10 minutes for medium and about 12 minutes for well done. Lift out the steak onto a warm plate, spoon off excess fat and add the brandy to the pan. Boil fiercely for a few seconds to drive off the alcohol and then stir in the cream. Cook together for a minute or two. Taste and add salt if necessary and pour over the steak.

Stir-Fry of Beef
(Serves 3-4)

Quick and tasty, ask the butcher for tender beef and cut it in fingerlike strips. Oyster Sauce which gives such a good flavour is available ready-made in small bottles.

1 large onion, chopped
1 - 2 cloves garlic, chopped
2 tablespoons butter
1 tablespoon oil
450g (1 lb) lean tender beef, cut in finger-like strips
175g (6oz) button mushrooms, quartered
110g (4oz) mangetout, chopped
2 tablespoons Oyster Sauce
3 tablespoons cream
Half teaspoon mustard
Salt and freshly ground black pepper

Using a large frying pan or wok, fry the onion and garlic in half the butter and oil until soft. Lift out. Add in the beef in two lots and fry until just cooked. Lift out and wipe pan. Add in the remaining oil and butter, then the mushrooms and mangetout. Toss and fry together until soft, then add the oyster sauce, cream, mustard and the onions and beef. Fry together for a minute or two. Add salt and pepper to taste. Serve immediately.

Country Terrine

(Serves 5 - 6 for light meal or 8 as a starter)

This tasty, coarse-textured terrine (pâté) includes pork and prunes in the list of ingredients. Prunes are dried plums and the French particularly love their succulent 'pruneaux d'Agen' from the south-west of France.

Prunes, like other dried fruits, are high in fibre and contain some iron, potassium and vitamin A. Interestingly, prunes also contain traces of an element (hydroxyphenylisatin) that does stimulate parts of the intestine, so there is some truth in the rumour!

Terrines make nice cold meals or if served in small slices are suitable as a starter.

275g - 350g (10 - 12 oz) streaky rashers (smoked if preferred)
450g (1 lb) lean pork pieces
1 medium onion, quartered
2 cloves garlic, chopped
2 slices bread
1 joint of duck (can be bought fresh or frozen)
250g (9oz) large prunes
Salt and freshly ground black pepper
50g (2oz) walnuts, chopped

Tin: Loaf tin 23cm x 12.5cm x 7.5cm (9" x 5" x 3" deep).

Preheat Oven: Moderate oven (180°C, 350°F, Gas 4).

Cooking Time: About 1¼ to 1½ hours.

First prepare the tin by lining it with overlapping streaky rashers. Retain 50g (2oz) of the rashers for the mixture itself.

Put the pork pieces (in two or three lots) into the food processor and buzz to chop finely and then transfer to a mixing bowl. Next buzz the onion, garlic and rashers with the bread until coarsely chopped. Add to the pork. (If no food processor is available, simply chop the ingredients finely.)

Remove the skin and bones from the duck. Chop the flesh and buzz for a few seconds in the food processor, adding it also, to the pork. Remove the stones from the prunes and chop coarsely, adding to the meat mixture. Season well with salt and pepper. Finally, add chopped walnuts. Mix everything thoroughly together. (I find using my hands, in disposable gloves, the most effective way to mix.) Spoon the mixture into the prepared tin and spread evenly out. Cover the top with foil. Stand the tin in a roasting tin half filled with boiling water. Put in the oven to cook until done.

To check if cooked, pierce right into the centre with a skewer, catch the juices that run out, in a spoon. They should be clear or golden and not pink. If pink, continue cooking.

Lift the loaf tin out of roasting tin. Do **not** pour off the juices. Cover the top with greaseproof paper or foil, place something heavy on top and leave to cool overnight. Remove weight, cover and keep the terrine, in the fridge, for a day or two to allow the flavours to mellow nicely together. The terrine has a lovely coarse, mottled appearance with the walnuts adding a gentle crunch to the texture.

Pork and Cider Stir-Fry (Serves 4)

Pork makes a tasty and satisfying stir-fry. The vegetables have an attractive green colour.

1 pork steak
2 - 4 tablespoons oil
Half onion, chopped
1 clove garlic, chopped
1 leek, washed and sliced
1 small courgette, diced
2 sticks celery, chopped
1 crisp eating apple, chopped

Sauce:
1 heaped teaspoon cornflour
150ml (quarter pt) cider
1 - 2 tablepoons soy sauce
1 teaspoon grated fresh root ginger (optional)
2 teaspoons chutney (optional)
1 teaspoon sugar
Salt and freshly ground black pepper

To Serve: Chopped fresh chives

Cut the pork steak into thin slices, and if liked cut each slice in half. Fry, a little at a time, in some of the oil, until cooked through. Drain the meat on paper towels. Wipe out the pan (or wok) and put in fresh oil. Fry the onion, garlic, leek, courgette and celery until golden and softened a little. Add the apple and cook everything for a few minutes.

Mix together all the sauce ingredients, add to the vegetables. Add the cooked pork. Season with salt and pepper, if necessary. Bring to the boil, stirring and tossing until the sauce thickens. Serve as soon as possible, scattered with chopped fresh chives.

Accompany with boiled rice.

Scalloped Ham (or Bacon) and Potatoes (Serves 4 - 5)

This looks rather like a lasagne and is a tasty way to serve left over bacon or ham, layered with sliced cooked potatoes and a tasty sauce, and baked until golden brown.

900g (2 lb) steamed (or boiled) potatoes
275 - 350g (10 - 12oz) cooked ham or bacon
1 onion, chopped
1 - 2 tablespoons oil
1 - 2 leeks, washed and thinly sliced
2 sticks celery, thinly sliced
4 rings pineapple, cut in chunks (optional)
Salt and freshly ground black pepper
Pinch mixed herbs

Sauce:
570ml (1 pt) milk
50g (2oz) margarine
50g (2oz) flour
Salt and freshly ground black pepper
Half teaspoon mustard
25g (1oz) grated cheese - (optional)

For the top:
50g (2oz) grated cheese (mixture of cheddar and mozzarella)

Dish: Lasagne dish, greased

Preheat Oven: Moderately hot oven 190°C, 375°F, Gas 5.

Cooking Time: About 30 - 45 minutes.

Peel and slice the potatoes. Cut the ham into small slices. Fry the onion until soft in the oil adding in the thinly sliced leeks, celery and pineapple chunks. Season lightly with pepper, salt and a pinch of mixed herbs. Fry lightly for a minute or two.

Sauce: Make the sauce using the following speedy method - put all the sauce ingredients - except the cheese into a saucepan. Using a whisk , stir briskly over a gentle heat until the margarine melts and the flour is mixed through, then increase the heat and bring to a brisk boil (stirring all the time). Stir in the grated cheese and melt it.

Assemble the dish: Lightly grease the base of the lasagne dish and arrange a single layer of sliced potatoes over the bottom. Place the slices of ham on top and scatter the vegetable mixture in an even layer over the ham. Spoon one third of the sauce over the vegetables. Then cover the top with even, overlapping rows of the potato slices. Pour all the remaining sauce over them. Scatter the cheese over the surface. Bake until piping hot and golden brown on top.

Super Stuffed Pork Steak (Serves 3 - 4)

The delicious stuffing really gives great flavour and moisture to the pork steak.

1 large pork steak

Stuffing:
1 small onion, chopped
1 - 2 cloves garlic, crushed
175g (6oz) mushrooms
2 - 3 tablespoons olive oil
175g (6oz) rashers
Salt and freshly ground black pepper
Generous pinches sage or herbes de Provence
1 tablespoon finely chopped fresh parsley
Grated rind of half orange (optional)
Wooden cocktail sticks and fine string
2 - 3 tablespoons oil for frying

Preheat Oven: 190°C, 375°F, Gas 5.

Cooking Time: About 1 hour, after about 20 minutes reduce the heat to 170°C, 325°F, Gas 3.

Make the stuffing: Fry the onion, garlic and mushrooms together in the oil until they soften, then lift out with a perforated spoon. Next fry the rashers. When cooked drain on paper towels. Buzz the onions, mushrooms and rashers in a food processor to chop them very finely (almost like breadcrumbs). Add to the remaining stuffing ingredients and mix well together.

Slit the pork steak (without cutting right through), down the whole length. Fill with the stuffing and close back together, holding in position with the cocktail sticks and tie with string. Fry the pork steak as best you can to brown outside. Then place on foil on a roasting tin and wrap completely with the foil. Cook in the oven until tender. About 10 minutes before the end of cooking, open the foil and pour off the juices (add the juices to the gravy). Raise the temperature to 190°C, 375°F, Gas 5 to crisp and brown the outside.

Pork and Ham Loaf

This tasty meat loaf can be eaten hot or cold. The meats are minced in a mincer or a food processor.

Bacon can be used instead of ham.

Small joint of ham, about 700 - 900g (1½ - 2 lb) (see note)
350g (12oz) pork pieces (raw)
1 large onion, chopped finely
A little oil
2 cloves garlic crushed or chopped
1 medium cooking apple, grated
1 -2 sticks celery, finely chopped
75g (3oz) breadcrumbs (preferably wholemeal)
2 tablespoons chopped fresh parsley
1 teaspoon mustard
1 teaspoon oregano (or mixed herbs)
A few pinches nutmeg
Salt and freshly ground black pepper
2 eggs

To line the tin:
About 225g (8oz) rashers (optional)

Note: Raw ham or leftover baked ham (or boiled bacon) can be used.

To prepare the raw ham: Remove the skin and fat and cut the lean meat into large chunks (about 75g/3oz each). Put into a saucepan and cover with cold water. Bring gently to the boil and simmer for a few minutes. Then drain off the water. This pre-cooking is done to reduce the saltiness of the meat. You should now have about 450g (1 lb) of lean ham pieces.

If using baked ham: Less cooked ham (or boiled bacon) is required. Use 450g (1 lb) of the lean meat and cut into chunks. It requires no par boiling

Tin: Loaf tin, (23cm x 12.5cm/9" x 5"). Grease tin or line with the rashers laid side by side.

Preheat Oven: 200°F, 400°F, Gas 6.

Cooking Time: About 30 minutes. Then reduce the oven to 180°C, 350°F, Gas 4, and cook for another 30 - 45 minutes.

Mince the ham and mince the pork (a food processor is excellent for this but don't put in too much at one time or some of it will turn into gunge before the rest is minced). Put the meats together in a bowl. Fry the onion in a little oil until soft adding in the garlic. Add to the meats.

Add in all the other ingredients and mix thoroughly together. Spread evenly out in the prepared tin. Cover with foil. Stand in a baking tray to catch any juices that may escape. Cook in the centre of the oven. Remove the foil halfway through cooking.

To check if cooked, pierce right into the centre with a skewer, catch the juices that run out, in a spoon. They should be clear or golden and not pink. If pink continue cooking.

When cooked, if serving hot, pour the juices out of the loaf tin before turning out the meat loaf. Use the juices in the gravy or in a soup.

If serving cold, leave the juices and the meat loaf in the tin and allow to cool. When cold, turn out and serve.

Liver with Apple and Yogurt (Serves 2 - 3)

Liver is a very good source of iron, containing as it does about 13.5mg of iron per 100g. Dieticians encourage us to include it in our menus from time to time. Chopped onion and eating apple are fried with the liver. Natural yogurt (blended with a little cornflour) is added to the pan to make a tasty 'sauce'. These flavours compliment each other excellently. Liver should not be overcooked or it becomes tough. Increase ingredients as required.

4 pieces of calves liver (about 225g/8oz)
Flour, seasoned with salt and freshly ground black pepper
2 - 3 tablespoons oil
1 small onion, chopped
1 small eating apple, peeled and chopped
Salt and freshly ground black pepper
A few pinches of mixed herbs or thyme
1 rounded teaspoon cornflour
A little cold water
1 carton (125ml) natural yogurt

Wash the liver in plenty of lukewarm water, pat dry. Then dip each piece in the seasoned flour. Fry gently in the oil until cooked through, adding the onion and apple as it fries. Season with salt, pepper and the herbs.

Blend the cornflour with the water and stir in the yogurt.

The liver will be cooked by this stage so lift it out of the pan and keep warm.

Then pour the yogurt mixture into the pan and stir through the onion and apple mixture, bringing gently to the boil to thicken. Then add the liver back in and simmer everything together for a minute or two before serving.

Pork Medallions in Wine

(Serves 3 - 4)

The pork steak is thinly sliced into 'medallions', then fried and served in overlapping slices on top of this delicious vegetable and wine mixture.

1 small onion, chopped
1 clove garlic, chopped
Oil for frying
1 leek, thinly sliced
1 stick of celery, thinly sliced
1 carrot, finely diced
110g (4 oz) button mushrooms, sliced
2 tomatoes, chopped
1 glass wine (or cider)
1 small eating apple, peeled and diced finely (optional)
1 tablespoon soy sauce
Pork steak (about 350g/12 oz)
A little soy sauce, to brush
1 carton (75ml/3fl.oz) of fresh cream
Freshly ground black pepper
A little salt

Prepare the vegetables and apple. Heat a little of the oil (in a wok or wide saucepan) and fry the onion and garlic and when soft add in all the remaining vegetables and the apple, and fry gently for a few minutes. Then pour in the wine and soy sauce. Boil briskly for about 1 - 2 minutes, then cover with a lid and simmer for a few minutes until vegetables are tender. Check occasionally that the liquid doesn't cook off.

Meanwhile, slice the pork steak into thin slices ('medallions'). Brush these with a little extra soy sauce, and fry in two or three lots on a separate pan (using a little of the oil), until golden brown and cooked through.

Add the cream and pepper to the vegetables and cook together for about 2 - 3 minutes. Check the flavour and add salt if necessary.

Serve the vegetables and juices on 3 - 4 plates. Arrange the pork medallions in an overlapping row on top of the vegetables.

Accompany with potatoes, pasta or crusty bread.

Vegetables

Broccoli

When President Bush revealed that he hated broccoli, he threw the US broccoli growers into a state of panic, they loudly extolled the virtues of this tasty vegetable. It must be admitted though, that broccoli can be 'murdered' by over cooking to a mush, whilst others under-cook it, serving it virtually raw.

The broccoli normally available in the shops (correctly called calabrese because it was developed in Calabrese in Italy) consists of a compact head of green curds on one fat stalk. (Broccoli proper - consists of small heads each on individual stalks, too delicate for supermarket shopping !)

To prepare broccoli for cooking: I normally divide the broccoli into individual florets, but as I cut off each one, I continue cutting right down through the large stalk. This means that each floret has a thin long piece of stalk attached. Because it is thin the stalk will cook just as quickly as the rest.

Rinse the prepared broccoli in cold water. I prefer to steam broccoli, using my little 'rose petal steamer', as it requires the minimum amount of water underneath. Broccoli can also be cooked in the microwave, simply put the florets in a dish with a little salted water, cover with microwave cling film, pierce a few holes and cook on High for about 9 - 10 minutes per 450g (1 lb).

Orange 'n' White Sauce

For serving with broccoli.

250ml (Just under half pt) milk
25g (1oz) butter or margarine
25g (1oz) flour
1 small slice of onion
Salt and freshly ground black pepper
Juice 1 orange

Put all the ingredients, except the orange juice into a saucepan and stir briskly with a whisk while bringing to the boil. Then stir in the orange juice. Heat through and serve over the steamed broccoli.

Mustard Mayonnaise for Broccoli

A 'no-cook' sauce that is also very good to serve with cooked broccoli.

125ml (about 4fl.oz) mayonnaise
2 tablespoons fresh lemon juice
2 generous teaspoons French (Dijon) mustard
2 - 3 tablespoons fresh cream or yogurt

Simply mix all these ingredients together and serve.

Broccoli Purée in Tomato Cups   (Serves 4 - 5)

This makes a most attractive vegetable accompaniment. Ideal for situations where you want to prepare in advance. Easy to do and low in calories. Steamed broccoli is buzzed in a food processor to a purée. The purée is then filled into hollowed out beef tomatoes and baked.

450g (1 lb) broccoli
4 - 5 beef tomatoes
1 large egg
1 - 2 tablespoons mayonnaise or fresh cream
Salt and freshly ground black pepper
Half teaspoon French mustard
Generous pinch nutmeg
Grated Parmesan cheese (or cheddar and mozzarella)

Preheat Oven: 190°C, 375° F, Gas 5.

Cooking Time: About 20 - 25 minutes.

Cut the broccoli into florets, including some of the main stalk with each floret. Rinse in cold water and drain. Steam or boil florets until just tender. Meanwhile, cut the beef tomatoes in half, (horizontally to the stalk). Scoop out all the seeds (use them in a soup). Place the tomatoes, in a lightly greased oven proof dish.

When the broccoli is tender, buzz (in two or three lots) in a food processor. The purée will have a fine, grainy texture and a speckled green appearance. In a separate bowl, whisk together the egg, mayonnaise, and mustard. Then stir in the broccoli purée. Season with salt, pepper and nutmeg.

Spoon generously into the tomato cups and sprinkle the cheese on top. This much can be done in advance. Before serving, bake in the oven until the tomatoes are just tender and the broccoli is very slightly golden on top.

Broccoli Stir-Fry

(Serves 3 - 4)

Orange and broccoli are excellent together.

450g (1 lb) broccoli
1 clove garlic, chopped or crushed
1 orange, cut in segments (see note) (optional)
2 teaspoons oil

Sauce:
1 heaped teaspoon cornflour
Juice 1 orange plus enough water to make up 150ml (quarter pt)
1 - 2 tablespoons soy sauce
1 teaspoon brown (or white) sugar
Freshly ground black pepper

Cut the broccoli into florets, including some of the main stalk with each floret. Rinse, drain and steam or boil until almost tender.

Meanwhile make up the sauce by stirring all the ingredients together. Lightly fry the garlic using the oil, in a saucepan or wok.

Add the drained broccoli to the wok and pour in the sauce. Bring to the boil, stirring and tossing until sauce thickens. Add the orange segments (if using them) and cook gently until broccoli is bite-tender.

Note: To segment an orange: Peel the orange with a sharp knife, removing all the pith, so just the flesh shows. Carefully cut out each segment of orange from between the membranes (thin inner skin). Remove any pips.

Stir-Fried Sliced Sprouts

(Serves 4 - 5)

This tongue twister of a name accurately describes this dish which is a great way to serve sprouts. Quick to prepare and quick to cook.

450g (1 lb) sprouts
2 tablespoons butter
75ml (3fl.oz) water
1 clove garlic, crushed
Salt and freshly ground black pepper
Generous pinches mace OR nutmeg

Peel off any coarse outer leaves and trim stalk ends. Slice the sprouts very thinly, cutting across the little heads, rather than down the length. Rinse shredded leaves in cold water and drain well.

Put the butter and water into a pan or wide saucepan. Heat up and put in the garlic and the sprouts and cook for about 3 minutes. Remove the lid and cook off the water, by which time the sprouts should be nicely tender. Season with salt, pepper and mace. Serve immediately.

Stir-Fried Coleslaw (Serves 3 - 5)

There is no mayonnaise in this recipe! In fact I evolved this recipe because one day, making coleslaw I discovered I had no mayonnaise. It is a lovely fresh tasting vegetable dish.

Half - 1 small head cabbage (about 350g /12oz)
225g (8oz) carrots
1 medium leek
About 1 tablespoon olive oil
1 tablespoon butter
3 tablespoons water
Salt and freshly ground black pepper
Half tablespoon caraway seeds (optional)

A food processor is the ideal gadget to shred the cabbage and grate the carrots. If not available, shred the cabbage very finely and rinse quickly in a large bowl of cold water and put into a colander shake hard to get rid of the water. Wash, peel and grate the carrots. Mix the carrots and cabbage together.

Top and tail the leek and wash thoroughly, then slice very thinly. Heat the oil, butter and water in a wok or saucepan and fry the leek until soft but not browned. Add in the remaining vegetables also the seasoning and caraway seeds. Toss over a moderate heat, cover with a lid some of the time, and stir frequently until cooked by which time the water should have cooked off. Only takes about 5 minutes or so.

It is now well established that vegetables and fruit, by and large, play an important role in healthy eating, mainly they are very low in calories, as most contain lots of water and fibre. A very rough estimate is, that one would have to eat about 2 - 3 kg of vegetables to obtain 1000 calories. A mere 175g (6oz) of margarine or butter will give the same amount. Even potatoes are included in this group - needless to say they would be served plain without any delicious lumps of butter on top!

All vegetables contain valuable amounts of vitamin C (ascorbic acid) though the quantities are variable and they do reduce during cooking and preparation. Vegetables (and fruit) are at their best when just picked or harvested. So buy as fresh as you can. Chopping and slicing vegetables (and fruit) releases an enzyme which, ironically, helps to destroy the vitamin C content - so ideally don't prepare the vegetables too far in advance of eating.

We are encouraged to include at least 4 - 5 servings of fruit or vegetables everyday.

Autumn has really come when you see the curly kale in the shops! Kale was originally a Scottish word for cabbage, but now the name applies to that open-headed variety of cabbage with the dark, very curly leaves. Dark, green leafy vegetables contain traces of iron, calcium, vitamin A, vitamin D and of course are very low in calories. Curly kale is an important ingredient in the traditional Hallowe'en dish - Colcannon - though many people prefer to use cabbage instead. The positive flavour of the curly kale is best blended with other ingredients rather than eaten on its own. When buying curly kale, buy it as fresh and crisp as possible. However, a limp head (or stalks) can be restored by cutting off the ends of the stalk(s) and standing in cold water to give them a good drink.

Curly Kale

To Prepare: Cut off the individual leaves and wash well. Then cut away and discard the thick 'rib' that runs up the centre of each leaf. If necessary, discard any discoloured leaves. Shred the leaves very thinly with a sharp knife.

To Cook: Use a wide, heavy-based saucepan, as this allows as much of the vegetable to come in touch with the heat as possible, and requires the minimum amount of water. Put about 2.5 cm (1") of water in the base of the saucepan and add in the prepared curly kale. Season with **salt and freshly ground black pepper and a few pinches of sugar.** Put on the lid and bring to the boil and simmer for about 8 - 10 minutes, check that the water doesn't boil off. Drain off any remaining water (ideally use it in a gravy). Cooking reduces the bulk of the vegetable by about half. The kale is ready now to use in the following tasty dish.

Baked Curly Kale Dish   (Serves 3)

The cooked curly kale is mixed with some white sauce. An egg yolk is also added. The egg white is beaten until stiff and mixed through. The mixture, is then sprinkled with Parmesan cheese and baked in the oven.

550g (1¼ lb) curly kale - yields 225g (8oz) prepared leaves

Sauce :
275g (half pint) milk
25g (1oz) margarine
25g (1oz) flour
1 slice onion
Salt and freshly ground black pepper
Pinches mace
Pinches mixed herbs
1 large egg, separated
1 tablespoon Parmesan cheese

Preheat Oven: 200°C, 400°F, Gas 6.

Cooking Time: About 20 minutes.

Prepare and cook the curly kale as described on page 84.

Meanwhile, make a speedy white sauce as follows - put the milk, margarine and flour into a saucepan. Add the onion and seasoning. Using a whisk, stir briskly, while bringing to the boil to thicken. Add the cooked, drained curly kale to this sauce. Flavour with the mace and mixed herbs. Discard the slice of onion. (At this stage, I like to put the mixture into a food processor and buzz for a few seconds. This gives a finer texture - but it is optional.) Mix the yolk of the egg into the mixture.

Whisk the large egg white, in a bowl, until stiff and then stir gently into the sauce mixture. Put into a greased ovenproof dish. Scatter the cheese over the top. Bake until it puffs up a little and turns a golden brown. Serve as soon as possible.

Milky Microwave Spuds

(Serves 3- 4)

I love potatoes cooked in milk - but when cooked in a saucepan, the milk burns easily and cleaning the saucepan afterwards can be a nuisance. Cooking them in the microwave eliminates this problem. However, a large bowl is essential as the milk froths right up and will spill over. I use a pyrex mixing bowl. Also I use floury potatoes.

550 - 700g (1¼ - 1½ lb) potatoes
225ml (8fl.oz) low fat milk
Knob butter
Salt and freshly ground black pepper,
1 - 2 tablespoon chopped fresh parsley

Peel, wash and cut the potatoes into cubes (for speed use a chip cutter). Incidentally, don't wash the potatoes **after** they have been chopped, as this will remove the natural starch which thickens the milk. Put potatoes into the large bowl. Pour in the milk. Cover the bowl with cling film, piercing a few holes in the centre.

Cook for 5 minutes on HIGH and then take out and stir. Return to the microwave and cook for another 5 minutes on HIGH. It is during this second cooking that the heat will have penetrated the potatoes and the milk starts to froth. (If your bowl is not big enough, stand it on a plate, which will catch any milk that spills over, so it can be poured back in at the end.) Repeat the stirring and test for tenderness. Return for another 3 - 5 minutes on HIGH, or until potatoes are just tender. Add the butter, seasonings and parsley into the potatoes and mash with a potato masher. The consistency will be soft and the taste will be delicious.

Mushrooms and Courgette Kebabs (Serves 3 - 4)

Mushrooms and courgettes are made very flavoursome by marinating them in one of the following marinades, before cooking. Incidentally, small plastic freezer bags make really handy containers in which to hold the marinating vegetables. Closed tightly with a wire closure, the bags store easily in the fridge and can be shaken every now and then to ensure the marinade soaks evenly through.

350g (12oz) button mushrooms, wiped clean.
OR 350g (12oz) courgette, cut in chunks

Steep them in one of the following marinades;

Marinade with Lemon and Herbs:
5 tablespoons oil - preferably olive oil
2 tablespoons lemon juice
Salt and freshly ground black pepper
1 teaspoon sugar
Quarter teaspoon herbes de Provence, or oregano
2 cloves garlic, crushed

OR

Marinade with Pesto:
5 tablespoons olive oil
2 tablespoons wine vinegar
Salt and freshly ground black pepper
1 tablespoon Pesto (available in small jars)
1 clove of garlic, crushed

Mix the marinade ingredients together and transfer to a plastic bag with the mushrooms or courgettes. Shake occasionally and leave for at least half an hour before threading onto skewers and cooking under the grill or over a barbecue.

Spinach and Mushrooms Au Gratin (Serves 3)

A speedily prepared dish that 'dresses up' frozen spinach very successfully. The cooked spinach is topped with a shallow layer of fried mushrooms, then grated cheese is sprinkled over the top and it is grilled lightly.

225g (8oz) frozen leaf spinach, thawed
25g (1oz) butter, melted
Salt and freshly ground black pepper
Generous pinches nutmeg
110g (4oz) mushrooms, sliced
1 tablespoon olive oil
1 clove garlic, chopped
25g (1oz) cheddar cheese and mozzarella, grated
2 - 3 teaspoons Parmesan cheese

Put the thawed spinach into a saucepan with the butter. Season with salt and pepper and nutmeg. Stir over a moderate heat until heated through. Transfer to a hot ovenproof dish and keep warm.

Meanwhile fry the mushrooms in the oil with the garlic until soft and lightly golden. Season lightly with a little salt and pepper. Place in a layer over the spinach. Sprinkle the cheeses over the top. Grill until the cheeses start to melt nicely, then serve.

Note: If you would prefer to use fresh spinach, use 450g (1 lb) fresh spinach, and follow the preparation and cooking instructions, as described in Spinach Soup on page 10.

Vegetable Goulash

(Serves 4 - 5)

Low in calories. The combination of vegetables can be varied to suit personal taste. Don't be put off by the list of ingredients, they are all very simple. The addition of cayenne pepper gives a nice 'kick' to the flavour. Serve the goulash with crusty bread or potatoes.

2 onions, chopped
3 tablespoons olive oil
2 cloves garlic, chopped
175g (6oz) mushrooms sliced
1 heaped teaspoon paprika
Quarter - half teaspoon cayenne pepper
1 tin chopped tomatoes
1 tablespoon tomato purée
350g (12oz) carrots, thinly sliced
3 sticks celery, chopped
1 red and/or 1 green pepper, chopped
275 - 570ml (½ - 1 pt) vegetable stock, (use cube if necessary)
Salt and freshly ground black pepper
1 tin red kidney beans, drained
2 - 3 heaped teaspoons cornflour

To serve: Greek style yogurt

Using a heavy-based saucepan large enough to hold all the ingredients, fry the onion in the oil (adding in the garlic) until soft. Add in the mushrooms and continue frying until they are softish. Add the paprika and cayenne pepper. Stir in the chopped tomatoes and tomato purée. Add in all the remaining ingredients (except the kidney beans), using only enough stock to barely cover the vegetables. Stir well and bring to the boil. simmer gently with the lid on for about 30 - 40 minutes until the carrots are tender. About 10 minutes before the end of cooking time add the red kidney beans and the cornflour blended with a little water. Bring to the boil stirring, then simmer for a while.

Serve with yogurt.

To cook in oven: Do the initial preparation on a frying pan - to the stage of adding the tin of chopped tomatoes - then transfer to a casserole, adding all the remaining ingredients. Cover with a tight fitting lid and cook for about 1 hour in a moderate oven (180°C, 350°F, Gas 4) .

Picture opposite: Fruity Cider Muffins

Overleaf Left: Quick Open Apple Tart

Overleaf Right: Fillets of Sea Trout Stuffed with Mushrooms and Bacon

Gratin of Winter Root Vegetables (Serves 4 - 6)

The real joy of 'gratin' is the contrast between the crusty top and the delicious, soft interior - with the added satisfaction of scraping off the lovely crusty bits around the edge. The modern interpretation of 'au gratin' is cooked food covered with a sauce, topped with grated cheese or bread crumbs and browned under the grill. However, the traditional and probably the best way to cook 'au gratin' is to bake the dish slowly in the oven. The Savoy and Dauphin regions of France (the mountainous Alps to the east of Lyons) are the areas where these delicious gratin dishes were traditionally developed. No doubt the hardy winters there, had something to do with it.

The best traditional gratins are made with potatoes and other starchy vegetables such as carrots and parsnips. The dish needs minimum attention and is ideal for putting in the oven with a roast or casserole. It can even be cooked the night before, and reheated quickly the next day when you 'flop' home exhausted and starving.

Your choice of vegetables can vary according to taste, but the weight of the potatoes should be equal to the combined weights of the other vegetables used. Wash after peeling but NOT after slicing, as this washes off the natural starch which helps thicken the juices.

500g (generous 1 lb) of potatoes
225g (8oz) carrots
225g (8oz) parsnip
2 cloves garlic, chopped finely
Salt and freshly ground black pepper
A few pinches of herbes de Provence
1 carton (170ml) fresh cream
Enough milk added to the cream to make 275ml (half pt)
50g (2oz) grated cheese (choose a mixture of cheddar and mozzarella)

Dish: Shallow ovenproof dish (or small roasting tin), greased thickly with butter or margarine.

Preheat Oven: 170°C, 325°F, Gas 3

Cooking Time: About 1½ to 2 hours

Peel, wash and slice all the vegetables very thinly. Arrange them in separate layers, finishing with potato, scattering the garlic, herbs and seasoning between each layer. Pour the mixed cream and milk over the lot and scatter the grated cheese on top. Bake in the upper part of a slow oven until tender.

If the oven is set at a higher temperature, because you are roasting meat at the same time, put the potatoes in the lower part, covering them with foil when they get brown enough.

Picture opposite: Broccoli Purée in Tomato Cups, Stir-Fried Coleslaw, Hot Potato Salad

Spiced Peppers and Potato Dish (Serves 4)

India is a vast country, but it's cuisine, like Europe, can be divided broadly into north and south. The north is a little cooler and wetter which favours the raising of cattle and the growing of wheat and this, naturally is reflected in it's dishes. The south on the other hand is notable for its use of vegetables, fruit and fish - much like the Mediterranean.

This tasty recipe uses familiar vegetables! Potatoes, peppers and onions, flavoured with curry powder.

450g (1 lb) potatoes, peeled and diced or chopped
3 tablespoons oil
1 large onion, sliced thinly
2 cloves garlic, chopped
2 tablespoons curry powder
1 tin chopped tomatoes
1 large red pepper, sliced with the seeds and stalk discarded
1 large green pepper, sliced with the seeds and stalk discarded
Salt and freshly ground black pepper
1 teaspoon sugar
1 teaspoon mustard seeds

To serve: Coriander or parsley

For convenience half cook the potatoes first by steaming or boiling. Put the oil into a pan and fry the onions and garlic until tender. Add the curry powder, stir it about. Stir over the heat for a minute or two and then add in the potatoes and the tin of tomatoes. Finally add in the peppers, salt, pepper, sugar and mustard seeds.

Cover with a lid and simmer gently with the lid on until the potatoes and peppers are tender. Check frequently, during cooking and if necessary add a small amount of water to prevent sticking. Serve hot (or cold) scattered with chopped fresh coriander.

Yogurt Accompaniment: Mix **1 - 2 tablespoons of mango chutney** with **250g (9fl.oz) of Greek style yogurt** and serve .

Hungarian Potatoes

(Serves 5 - 6)

Somewhat similar to the spiced Peppers and Potatoes, but paprika rather than curry powder is used and stock instead of chopped tomatoes.

700 - 900g (1½ - 2 lb) potatoes, peeled and chopped
3 tablespoons oil
2 - 4 rashers
1 large onion, chopped
2 cloves garlic, chopped
2 teaspoons paprika
275 - 570ml (half - 1 pt) chicken stock (or water and stock cube)
Salt and freshly ground black pepper
1 yellow or green pepper, chopped
2 - 3 tomatoes, chopped
1 pepperoni (or 4 cooked pork sausages)

To serve: Chopped fresh parsley

Dish: Use a wide based saucepan to cook this dish.

For speed half cook the potatoes by steaming or boiling them.

Fry the rashers in a little of the oil. Next fry the onion and garlic in fresh oil and when soft add in the paprika and take off the heat. Add the potatoes, rashers and just enough stock to come half way up the potatoes. (The potatoes are served in the stock, so it is important not to have too much.) Season with salt and pepper. Cover with a lid and bring to the boil. Simmer gently for about 5 - 10 minutes and then add in all the remaining ingredients. Continue cooking with the lid off until everything is tender, stirring occasionally.

Serve hot, scattered with chopped parsley - also good eaten cold!

Potato Wedges

A very handy way to cook potatoes in a hurry using a microwave.

4 medium/ large potatoes
Salt and freshly ground black pepper
50 - 75g (2 - 3 oz) grated cheese (see note)

Note: A combination of cheddar for flavour and mozzarella for 'meltability' is ideal.

Wash the unpeeled potatoes and cut in half (down the length) and then cut each half in half again - like wedges. (If potatoes are large, divide again.) Place these wedges of potatoes, close together on an ovenproof dish (skin-side downwards). Cover with a kitchen paper towel and cook on HIGH in the microwave for about 8 - 10 minutes or until they are just tender (if you don't have a microwave, boil the potatoes before cutting). Season them with salt and pepper and scatter the grated cheese generously over them. Grill until the cheese melts and turns golden. Serve hot.

Hot Potato Salad

(Serves 4 -5)

Wonderfully flavoursome. The hot potato salad is a lovely chunky mixture with onion, potatoes and lots of things. (A great way to reheat potatoes.)

5 - 6 rashers (back or streaky)
2 - 3 tablespoons oil
1 large onion, thinly sliced
2 - 3 cloves garlic, chopped
1 medium cooking apple (175g/6oz)
900g (2 lb) cooked potatoes, peeled and chopped
2 - 3 tablespoons vinegar
1 teaspoon sugar
Quarter teaspoon thyme
1 bay leaf
Salt and freshly ground black pepper
8 - 10 olives, green or black
1 tablespoon chopped fresh parsley

To serve: 4 - 6 teaspoons fromage frais OR dairy soured cream

Fry the rashers in 1 tablespoon of oil until cooked, then lift out and cut into strips. (Wipe the salty fat out of the pan.) Fry the onion in fresh oil, adding in the garlic. When soft add in the cooking apple and the potatoes, followed by all the other ingredients except the chopped parsley. Return the rashers to the pan and fry, stirring frequently, until everything is piping hot. Remove the bay leaf.

Scatter generously with the parsley and serve with the fromage frais.

Casseroled Potatoes

This is my version of the traditional Potato Savoyarde (sliced potatoes baked in stock). I love floury potatoes but these would crumble up if sliced, so I simply leave them whole. Pick even-sized potatoes and use enough to fit very tightly into whatever ovenproof dish you use. My preference is for narrow, oval shaped potatoes, which I stand on their ends in a casserole (cutting off a tiny slice to steady them). If the only available potatoes are round-shaped, choose a more shallow dish.

Approx. 900g (2 lb) or more, of even sized potatoes
275 - 570ml (½ - 1 pt) chicken stock (use a cube if necessary)
2 cloves garlic, finely chopped
Salt and freshly ground black pepper
2 bay leaves
2 whole cloves (the apple tart kind!)
25 - 50g (1 - 2oz) grated cheese, (choose a mixture of cheddar and mozzarella)

Dish: 1.75 litre (3 pt) casserole or ovenproof dish, greased

Preheat Oven: 180°C, 350°F, Gas 4.

Cooking Time: About 1 - 2 hours, depending on potato size.

Peel and wash the potatoes and fit them tightly into the dish. Pour in enough stock to come a little more than half way up the potatoes. Add in the remaining ingredients, scattering the cheese over the top. Bake uncovered in a slow oven until tender.

Potatoes contain carbohydrates, fibre, a very small amount of protein, some minerals (including potassium), and some vitamins (including vitamin C). Potatoes also contain a lot of water (they are about 70 - 80% water). As a result, the calorie content of potatoes is about 70 - 90 calories per 100g. However, if deep fried as chips the calorie content jumps to about 250 per 100g!

Because of the concentration of some vitamins and minerals just under the skin of potatoes, whenever possible cook potatoes unpeeled. Left-over potatoes can be made into snacks or used in recipes at a moments notice, particularly for hungry teenagers - so it is often handy to cook more than you need and they will keep in the fridge for a few days.

Despite the fact that I almost never make chips, my little gadget for cutting out the chips is constantly on the go - it is particularly handy if 'diced' potatoes are required in a recipe.

Skinning Peppers

If you find the flavour of raw peppers a bit too strong, try skinning them, as this really mellows their flavour .

Skinning peppers is not as simple as skinning tomatoes.

The first step is to cut the peppers in half and remove the seeds. Grill, with the skin side uppermost until the skin is blistered and blackened (OR hold over a gas flame.)

Put onto a plate and cover the peppers with a plate (or foil) to keep them moist as they cool, this helps to loosen the skins. Then scrape off the skin and rinse under a running cold tap to wash off all the little bits. Slice the peppers as required, discarding the stalks.

Pepper Salad $\hfill$ (Serves 3 - 4)

The wonderful colours of peppers look so good in salads. For a pepper salad, I prefer to remove the skins.

1 red pepper
1 green pepper
1 yellow pepper
A little finely chopped onion
Brown French dressing (page 100)

Skin the peppers as described above and cut into strips. Arrange the strips on a serving plate and scatter with the onion. Dribble the dressing all over the peppers. Leave to stand for about half an hour before serving.

Green Bean Salad Provençal $\hfill$ (Serves 4 - 5)

For a salad with a difference try this delicious Mediterranean style salad. Green beans are the main ingredient. Frozen green beans are suitable to use.

Serve the salad on a flat plate rather than in a bowl.

350g (12oz) green beans (frozen)
Half a bulb fennel
1 large beef tomato
6 - 8 black olives, chopped
1 tin anchovies, well drained and chopped
Basil or Tomato French Dressing (page 101)
Salt and freshly ground black pepper
1 tablespoon chopped fresh parsley

Cook the green beans according to the directions on the packet. Allow to get cold. Scatter them on the serving plate. Thinly slice the fennel and cut each slice into thin strips and scatter over the beans. Skin 1 beef tomato (immerse in boiling water for 1 minute to loosen the skin) and slice it. Then cut the slices into strips. These will not be very exact because of the shape of the tomato but in this way they will blend in better with the shape of the beans. Scatter on top of the other vegetables.

Next scatter the black olives and anchovies over everything. Dribble the dressing generously all over the salad. Season with salt and pepper, and scatter chopped parsley on top. Leave for about half an hour before serving, for the flavours to mingle. Accompany with crusty French bread when serving.

Red Kidney Bean Salad (Serves 4 - 5)

This salad has wonderful colour and great flavour. Serve as a light meal with crusty bread and lettuce or as a side dish. The beans are a good source of vegetable protein.

Tomato French Dressing (see page 101)
1 tin (400g/14oz) red kidney beans
Half cucumber, chopped
3 - 4 tomatoes, chopped
3 - 4 spring onions (scallions)
1 medium green or yellow pepper
4 - 8 green olives, stones removed (optional)
Salt and freshly ground black pepper
1 tablespoon chopped fresh parsley

First make the French dressing with the tomato flavouring.

Drain the kidney beans well and put into a salad bowl. Add the cucumber, tomatoes and the spring onions (scallions) to the beans. Chop the pepper, discarding the seeds and stalk and add to the beans with the olives, salt and pepper. Add the French Dressing to the salad and toss through. Leave to stand for a short while before serving. Scatter with a little chopped fresh parsley.

Creamy French Dressing

With all the ready made dressings available, why bother making your own ? This you cannot answer unless you actually try this delectable dressing for yourself! The little touch of fresh cream, adds that certain 'something' to the flavour. It will keep in the fridge for a couple of weeks.

The handy way to make French dressing, is to put all the ingredients into a jar with a lid. Then, before using, shake the jar vigorously to mix the ingredients together since they always separate when left to stand. If the lid is metal and there is any possibility of the vinegar reacting with it and causing rust, simply cover the top of the jar with cling film, before putting on the lid.

3 tablespoons olive oil (choose extra virgin with a good flavour)
3 tablespoons vegetable oil (I use corn or sunflower seed oil)
OR substitute the vegetable oil with all olive oil
3 tablespoons vinegar (cider or white wine vinegar)
1 - 2 tablespoons fresh lemon juice
1 - 2 cloves garlic, crushed
Salt and freshly ground black pepper
1 teaspoon sugar
Couple pinches of herbes de Provence
2 tablespoons fresh cream

Put the all ingredients together into a jar or jug. Mix well together before using on a salad. Try it on a potato or avocado or indeed any salad.

Brown French Dressing

Also a French dressing, but with a different emphasis, achieved by using a little soy sauce (or Worcestershire sauce) and no cream. This dressing has great flavour and is delicious on green and other salads.

3 tablespoons olive oil (choose extra virgin with a good flavour)
3 tablespoons vegetable oil (or olive oil)
3 tablespoons vinegar (preferably red wine vinegar)
1 teaspoon sugar
1 teaspoon mustard (English or French)
1 - 2 cloves garlic, crushed
2 teaspoons soy sauce OR Worcestershire Sauce
Freshly ground black pepper

Whisk or shake all the ingredients together.

Tomato French Dressing

Exactly the same as the Brown French Dressing except that **1 - 2 teaspoons of tomato purée** are added as well . This gives a nice richness to the colour and the taste. Particularly nice on tomato salads.

Fresh Basil Dressing

Fresh basil, with its fabulous aroma, makes a dressing that is wonderful with tomato or any Mediterranean style salad.

2 cloves garlic, crushed
4 - 5 leaves of fresh basil, finely chopped
5 tablespoons of olive oil (choose a tasty, extra virgin olive oil)
3 tablespoons vinegar (cider or wine vinegar)
Salt and freshly ground black pepper

Put everything into a jug or jar and whisk or shake together.

Yogurt and Basil (or Pesto) Dressing

Natural yogurt is a great stand-by for low calorie dressings. Fresh basil has a natural sweetness so no sugar is needed.

1 carton (125ml) natural yogurt
Juice half lemon
1 clove garlic, crushed
3 - 4 leaves fresh basil, finely chopped (see note)
Salt and freshly ground black pepper

Note: If fresh basil is not available, use 2 teaspoons of pesto sauce.

Whisk or shake all together and use within a few days.

Note to those who don't like garlic: Use a little bit of finely chopped onion instead of garlic in all the above dressings .

Cranberry Sauce

Bright fresh cranberries make a lovely sauce for turkey. This can be made a week or two in advance, but because the sugar content is not high enough it will not keep for months. Easy to make, this amount will fill about two 1 lb (450g) jam jars. Give one away as a gift?

1 medium onion, chopped
1 clove garlic, chopped
2 tablespoons olive oil
1 cooking apple (about 200g/7oz)
350g (12oz) packet fresh cranberries
150ml (quarter pt) water
75ml (3fl.oz) vinegar
175 - 225g (6 - 8 oz) sugar (brown or white)
Salt and freshly ground black pepper
Quarter teaspoon mixed spice
Quarter teaspoon oregano

Fry the onion and garlic in the oil until soft and then add in the peeled and chopped cooking apple and the cranberries. Pour in the water and vinegar. Cover with a lid and cook until the cranberries are just beginning to pop and become tender. Now add the sugar. Season with the salt and pepper. Also add the spice and oregano. Cook gently until the sugar dissolves and the mixture has a nice soft consistency. Put into spotlessly clean jars, cover and keep in a cool place.

Cranberry Salsa

Really delicious, it has a sharp, sweet, fruity flavour that is tasty with both hot and cold turkey and ham. No cooking- everything is raw !

350g (12oz) fresh raw cranberries
2 medium/large oranges
1 large eating apple, chopped
175 - 225g (6 - 8oz) caster sugar
Pinch nutmeg
1 - 2 tablespoons Irish Mist (optional)

Peel the oranges with a sharp knife to remove the skin and pith and chop roughly, removing any pips. Then simply buzz the oranges, cranberries, apple and sugar together in a food processor. Flavour with nutmeg and Irish Mist. This will keep for a few days, store in the fridge.

Desserts

Crusty Biscuit Base

If you don't enjoy making or cooking pastry you might like to try this really handy biscuit base. It consists of crushed biscuits and melted butter - like the base for a cheesecake - except that it has a raised edge all around and it is baked in the oven for a few minutes. This makes it lovely and crisp. It is not as solid as a pastry base but it is simple to make and it's crispness is particularly attractive in certain recipes. Fill as you wish.

225g (8oz) digestive biscuits
110g (4oz) melted butter (or margarine)
25g (1oz) caster sugar
Quarter teaspoon nutmeg

Tin: Round tin - preferably a spring-clip tin - (23cm/9" in diameter), greased.

Preheat Oven: 190°C, 375°F, Gas 5.

Cooking Time: 7 - 10 minutes.

Crush the biscuits very finely, add the butter, sugar and nutmeg, and mix. Put into the tin and spread over the base, pushing a little (about 1cm/ half" high) up the sides of the tin. Press crumbs firmly into position. Bake for about 7 - 10 minutes in a moderately hot oven until very slightly browned - don't let it burn! Leave to get **completely** cold in the tin, then open the spring clip, it can be left on the base of the tin or gently lifted off onto serving plate.

Banoffi Ice Cream   (Serves 5 - 6)

Rich and luscious - ideal for the occasional 'splurge'! The basic mixture is exactly the same as the one used for Banoffi Pie. Serve in small quantities - and then go for a quick jog !

Use the same ingredients as for the *toffee filling* in the Banoffi Pie (opp. page)
3 - 4 bananas, sliced
Juice half lemon
250ml (almost half pint) fresh cream, whipped

Prepare the toffee filling. When cooked add the sliced bananas and lemon juice and allow to cool. Then stir in the whipped cream. Put into a bowl into the freezer (or icebox at highest setting). When half frozen, take out and whisk briskly with an electric beater (to break down the ice crystals, this will also mash the bananas). Then return to the freezer to freeze completely. You can give a nice 'kick' to this ice cream, by including a splash of Rum when adding in the bananas.

Banoffi Pie

This tasty filling is made in a jiffy - **no** boiling tins of condensed milk for hours ! The flavour of the bananas, which are tossed in the lemon juice, makes a good contrast to the toffee. Don't count the calories!

Crusty Biscuit Base: (as on page 104)

Toffee filling:
75g (3oz) butter or margarine
50g (2oz) white sugar
75g (3oz) brown sugar
110g (4oz) golden syrup (see note)
110ml (4 fl.oz) fresh cream
Quarter teaspoon vanilla essence
3 - 4 bananas, sliced
Juice half lemon
150ml (5fl.oz) whipped sweetened cream

Note: Stand tin on scales and spoon out required weight.

Biscuit base: Gently remove the biscuit base from the spring-clip tin and place on a serving plate.

Toffee filling: Melt the butter in a heavy saucepan. Then add in the sugars and syrup. Stir over a gentle heat until the sugars dissolve. Add in the cream. Bring the mixture to the boil and boil gently for about 3 - 5 minutes. It is not possible to be too exact about length of boiling time - too little means the toffee will be very soft, too much and it will be too stiff. Test if cooked enough, by putting a small teaspoonful of the syrup on a cold saucer and placing it in the ice box or fridge to cool quickly. If ready, the toffee will thicken and lose it's runny quality within a minute or two (while doing this test, take the saucepan off the heat to prevent further cooking). The toffee stiffens as it cools. If too runny, it can be cooked more. If too stiff, a little extra cream can be added. Add the vanilla essence. Pour the toffee mixture into the biscuit base and allow to cool. Toss the sliced bananas in lemon juice and arrange on top of the cooled toffee filling. Decorated generously with whipped sweetened cream.

Tarte Tatin

This is a classic French recipe for an upside-down apple tart!

What makes it special is that wedges of apples are first tossed in hot caramel, before being put into the tin and covered with pastry and baked. The pastry absorbs some of the caramel during baking. The sharp, fresh flavour of the apples combines excellently with the sweet of the caramel and the crunch of the pastry. It is nicest served warm rather than hot. Accompany with cream, or even better still, use creme fraîche (dairy soured cream).

If you are counting calories - forget it !!

Ground Almond Pastry:
150g (5oz) flour
50g (2oz) ground almonds
25g (1oz) caster sugar
75g (3oz) butter or margarine
About 3 tablespoons water

Apples:
900g (2 lb) eating apples (Granny Smiths)
A little lemon juice

Caramel:
110g (4oz) sugar
4 tablespoons water
A knob of butter (optional)

Tin: Sandwich tin or a pyrex pie plate (23cm/9")in diameter, greased.

Preheat Oven: 190°C, 375°F, Gas 5.

Cooking Time: About 25 - 35 minutes.

Pastry: Put the first three ingredients into a bowl. Add the butter cut into lumps and rub into the flour mixture (or buzz for a few seconds, in the food processor) until it looks like fine breadcrumbs. (Be careful if using a food processor not to over-buzz and cause the crumbs to form a dough. Turn crumbly mixture out into a bowl.) Then add just enough water to bind the ingredients together. Gather into a ball, cover and keep to one side. No need to chill (because if cold it is inclined to crack when rolled out).

Apples: Granny Smith apples are a good choice because of their sharp flavour and firm flesh. Peel and put the whole apples into a bowl of water. Then pat each apple dry and cut each into quarters or eighths depending on size (removing the core). (Wedges should be about 2.5cm/1" thick at the widest side.) Don't return wedges to the water or they will get too wet. Put into a separate bowl, and sprinkle with the lemon juice.

Caramel: A heavy-based saucepan is important. I like to choose a big, deep saucepan, in case of splashes. Also, do note that even though it may seem to take a while for the caramel to turn golden, when it does the golden colour will very quickly turn to dark brown and become very bitter. So having the apples ready to add to the caramel at the right point stops the caramel turning any darker. The apples also add moisture to the caramel and prevent it from setting hard.

Put the sugar into the saucepan with the water. Stir over a gentle heat until the sugar dissolves. Then boil, without stirring, until the sugar starts to turn golden . Lower the heat and swirl the saucepan once or twice, so that the syrup colours evenly. As soon as it has turned a nice golden colour - stand well back - and add in the prepared apples . They will splutter like crazy for a minute (this is why I use the big deep saucepan).

Simmer the apples gently in the caramel for a few minutes to allow the flavours to mingle. If you like you can add the butter, but it is not essential.

To assemble: Arrange the apples neatly in the base of the prepared tin, remembering that, when turned out, this will be the top. Pour remaining caramel on top of the apples. Roll the pastry out into a circle, so that it is about 2.5cm (1") larger than the tin. Place the pastry over the top and tuck in the pastry around the edges - as if you are making the apples nice and comfy! This will be the border of the tart when it is turned out.

To bake: Bake in the upper part of the oven until the pastry is a nice golden colour and well cooked. Leave to stand in the tin for a short while to 'settle' before turning out.

To turn out, put the serving plate over the tin and holding the two, firmly together, invert them. Gently lift off the tin, giving time for any pieces of apple that might stick, to loosen.

Serve warm. (If making in advance, don't turn out the tart until nearer to serving, warming it first in the oven before hand, to loosen the caramel).

Apples in Caramel

The apples cooked in the caramel are just delicious. Forget all about the pastry in the above recipe and simply serve the apples, prepared and cooked in the caramel exactly as described above for the Tarte Tatin.

They can be eaten either hot or cold, served with ice cream, cream or crème fraîche.

Fresh Pineapple in Caramel

Peeled and sliced fresh pineapple makes a delicious alternative to the apples cooked in the caramel. Use 1 whole pineapple, peeled and sliced.

Caramel Sauce

Make a delicious sauce with the caramel. Use the recipe for caramel in the Tarte Tatin (previous page).

Cook the sugar and water to the required colour exactly as described. Draw off the heat as soon as it reaches the right colour and immediately pour in 150ml (5fl.oz) fresh cream - being sure to stand well back. Stir over a gentle heat to mix the cream through the caramel. Serve hot or cold. Use it with ice cream, poached pears or whatever you fancy.

Oranges in Red Wine   (Serves 5 - 6)

A left over glass of wine can be made into a very tasty dessert.

1 glass red wine
1 glass water
About 110g (4oz) caster sugar
1 cinnamon stick OR quarter teaspoon ground cinnamon
2 whole cloves
2 wedges of lemon
4 - 5 large oranges

Put the wine, water, sugar and cinnamon into a saucepan. Stick the cloves into the lemon and add to the wine. Bring to the boil, stirring to dissolve the sugar and simmer for about 3 minutes. Meanwhile, using a sharp knife, peel the oranges (saving any escaping juices). Cut into slices, across, and add to the wine mixture. Allow to cool and serve cold with cream.

Picture opposite: Beef Olives

Overleaf Left: Pork Medallions in Wine

Overleaf Right: Brenda's Fruit and Nut Ring Cake

Quick Open Apple Tart

(Serves 6)

I have evolved this French-style apple tart that is really quick to prepare. It consists simply of a flat sheet of puff pastry, topped with jam and apple slices. The margin of pastry left around the edge - puffs up delightfully when cooked.

225g (8oz) frozen puff pastry OR ready-rolled puff pastry (thawed)
2 - 3 tablespoons blackcurrant jam
2 rounded teaspoons cornflour
2 large cooking apples (Bramley)
A little melted butter
1 teaspoon caster sugar

Tin: Flat baking tin, greased lightly.

Preheat Oven: 200°C, 400°F, Gas 6.

Cooking Time: About 25 - 35 minutes.

Roll out the pastry - (or cut ready-rolled pastry) - to approx. 25.5cm x 30.5cm (10" x 12") and place on greased tin. Blend the jam thoroughly into the cornflour and spread in a layer over the pastry - leaving a margin of about 2.5cm/1" all around the edge (the blackcurrant gives a positive colour). Peel the cooking apples. Cut them in half and remove the core. Then continue cutting the apples into quarters, then into eighths and so on until the wedges of apple are about 1cm/half" thick on their 'fat' side. Now lay the apples, in overlapping rows on top of the jam - still leaving the margin of pastry visible round the edge. Brush the apples lightly with a little melted butter and sprinkle very lightly with the caster sugar (remember it is the jam that provides the necessary sweetness).

Bake in the upper part of the oven. When cooked the margin of pastry will have puffed up all around the apples and the apples will be tender. Serve hot or warm.

With approximately 5 mg of vitamin C (ascorbic acid) in every 100g - apples rate very poorly compared to blackcurrants - which contain about 200mg in every 100g. But then how often do we eat blackcurrants? A little and often is much more beneficial, and this is how apples feature in most of our diets. It is interesting to note that the highest concentration of vitamin C in the apple is close to the skin and likely to be removed with peeling. For the record, oranges contain about 50mg of vitamin C in every 100g.

Together with their vitamin C content apples also provide us with a source of natural sugar and of fibre. Since they contain a lot of water their calorie content is quite low - 100g of apples contains about 46 calories, compared to about 580 calories in the same weight of milk chocolate!

Picture opposite: Chocolate Bakewell Tart with Blackberry Sauce

Poached Plums and Pears

Plums and pears are cut in quarters and poached in orange juice, sweetened with sugar and spices. For preference choose the dark blue plums, because their lovely golden coloured flesh and red juice, gives great colour to the dish. This is equally good eaten hot or cold. Ideally, both fruits should be at the same stage of ripeness. If not, start poaching the less ripe one a little bit before the other.

450g (1 lb) plums
3 - 4 pears
Juice 2 oranges
Water
50g (2oz) sugar
Quarter teaspoon allspice (or mixed spice)

Wash the plums, cut in halves, and remove the stones. Peel the pears, then quarter them (down the length) and remove the core.

Put the orange juice in a little saucepan, with enough water to make up half a pint. Don't be generous with the water because the fruit is juicy anyway. Add the sugar and allspice. Heat to partially dissolve the sugar and then add in the fruit. Use a wide-based saucepan so that most of the fruit will be in touch with the base. Cover with a lid and bring to the boil, then reduce the heat right down and simmer very gently (so the fruit keeps its shape) until it is tender. Sweeten with a little extra sugar if necessary. Serve on its own or accompany with cream or strawberry flavoured yogurt.

Oranges are native to China. It was Arab traders who first introduced oranges to Europe via Spain. Although available all year round, oranges and other citrus fruits are particularly plentiful after Christmas. Happily, modern transportation allows us enjoy these sunshine fruits in the depths of winter. Oranges are appreciated for their good vitamin C (ascorbic acid) content. In the seventies great claims were made that large quantities of vitamin C would cure or prevent the common cold, though there has been little clinical evidence to prove this. Nevertheless, vitamin C plays a very important role in our overall health. We are constantly being advised to eat plenty of fresh fruit and vegetables. What could be easier than to peel and eat an orange.

When buying oranges choose healthy, smooth ones that feel heavy in the hand for their size.

Fresh Orange Sauce

Fresh oranges are used to make this lovely fresh tasting sauce. Suitable for serving with many desserts such as ice cream or Banana Rolls.

4 oranges
Water
1 level tablespoon cornflour
75g (3oz) caster sugar
A few drops vanilla essence

Peel two of the oranges with a sharp knife, removing all the pith and membrane, so just the flesh shows. Carefully cut out each segment of orange from between the membranes (thin inner skin). A sharp knife is necessary. Work over a plate or bowl to catch the juices that escape.

Squeeze the juice from the 2 remaining oranges and add enough water to make half a pint. Blend the cornflour with a small drop of water and add to the orange juice and water along with the sugar and the vanilla essence. Bring to the boil in a saucepan to thicken, stirring all the time. Add the prepared orange segments and juices. Heat them through in the sauce. Serve hot or cold.

Three Melon Salad   (Serves 5 - 6)

For best effect use three different coloured melons.

The water melon provides the lovely red colour flesh, and a galia melon provides pale green flesh while the honeydew melon provides the creamy, white flesh. Ideally, use a Melon Baller (potato ball cutter), to scoop out the flesh of the melons in little 'ball' shapes. To be economical, cut out each shape really close to the previous one. Don't try to get perfect ball shapes everytime or there will be far too much waste. A low claorie dessert.

Half water melon, depending on size
1 galia melon
Half / 1 honeydew melon
110g (4oz) green grapes,
A hint of sugar !
Small sprig fresh thyme or rosemary (optional)

Cut the flesh of the melons with the melon baller. Do this over a bowl to catch the escaping juices. Discard the black seeds from the watermelon. Unless using seedless ones, cut the grapes in half and remove the seeds. Mix everything together in a serving bowl, including any juices. Before serving remove the herbs.

Nectarine or Peach Pie

(Serves 5 - 6)

Just like an apple tart. Particularly suitable for slightly under-ripe nectarines or peaches, that you haven't the patience to wait to ripen!

1 packet frozen shortcrust pastry, thawed (or make your own shortcrust pastry)

Filling:
700g (1½ lb) peaches or nectarines
50g (2oz) caster sugar
1 tablespoon flour
Generous pinches of cinnamon
Generous pinches of nutmeg
Seeds from the centre of 2 cardamom pods, crushed (optional but nice).

For the top (optional):
Half of 1 beaten egg
50g (2oz) chopped almonds

Tin: Sandwich tin or pie plate 21.5cm/8½" in diameter, greased

Preheat Oven: 200°C, 400°F, Gas 6.

Cooking Time: 35 - 45 minutes.

There is no need to skin the nectarines or the peaches. However, if you'd prefer, they can be skinned in the same way as tomatoes - simply pour boiling water over them and leave to stand for about 15 seconds or longer depending on the ripeness of the peach, then peel off the skins.

Cut the peaches or nectarines in half and remove the stones, then cut each half in slices (about 1.5cm/threequarters" thick), put them in a bowl. Add all the remaining filling ingredients to the fruit and toss together.

Roll out two-thirds of the pastry and line the greased tin. Put in the filling and then roll out the remaining pastry to cover the top. Seal the edges well by dampening them with water. Brush the top with the beaten egg and scatter with the chopped almonds. Pierce a few holes in the top to release the steam.

Place in the upper part of the oven with a tin on the shelf underneath to catch any juices, should they spill out (save the dreaded oven cleaning job). Bake until the pastry is well cooked. If your oven is a hot one, you may need to reduce the heat somewhat during the cooking.

Allow the pie to stand for at least half an hour before slicing it. Dust the top with icing or caster sugar.

Banana Rolls

This makes a delightful dessert that can be served hot or cold.

1 packet frozen shortcrust pastry
3 - 4 bananas, as straight as possible!
2 - 3 tablespoons brown sugar
1 teaspoon finely grated orange rind
A few pinches of cinnamon
A few pinches of nutmeg
If you have them - use the seeds from a few cardamom pods
1 egg , beaten (or milk)
About 40g (1½ oz) chopped almonds

Tin: Baking tin , lightly greased.

Preheat Oven: 200°C, 400°F, Gas 6.

Cooking Time: 25 - 30 minutes.

Roll out the thawed shortcrust pastry into a long strip. The strip should be a little bit wider than the length of the bananas. Mix the sugar, orange rind and the spices, put on a board. Place each banana, one at a time onto the mix, pressing well and rolling it back and forth, with the hand. This not only makes the sugar mixture stick, but it will also "straighten" the banana. (A curved banana may crack, but don't worry, it won't be noticed inside the pastry.) Place a sugared banana at the end of the pastry strip, roll up, cutting it to fit. Moisten the edges, leaving the join underneath. Seal at each end. Brush the top with a little beaten egg or milk and scatter some of the chopped almonds on top and place on the tin. Prepare each banana in the same way. Bake until golden brown.

Serve hot or cold, plain or with fresh cream. Orange Sauce or Caramel Sauce make good alternatives.

Chocolate Bakewell Tart

(Serves 5 - 6)

Delicious. Serve as a dessert or cake. A blackberry (or raspberry) sauce with it's lovely sharp flavour, combines excellently with the rich chocolate of the tart. No need to pick the blackberries - frozen ones will do.

Pastry Base:
Frozen shortcrust pastry will do. For a special occasion use the Ground Almond Pastry, (see Tarte Tatin on page 106).

Filling:
Apricot jam
75g (3oz) melted dark chocolate (good quality)
75g (3oz) butter or margarine
75g (3oz) caster sugar
75g (3oz) ground almonds
1 large egg
Half teaspoon almond essence

Tin: Sandwich tin 21.5 - 23cm (8½ - 9") in diameter, greased.

Preheat Oven: 200°C, 400°F, Gas 6.

Cooking Time: Bake in the upper part of the oven, after 10 minutes reduce the heat to 180°C, 350°F, Gas 4 and continue baking for about another 30 minutes or until the chocolate mixture is cooked.

Base: Roll out the pastry and line the prepared tin, trimming off the excess pastry.

Filling: Spread a layer of apricot jam over the pastry base.

Melt the chocolate. In a separate bowl, beat the butter until soft and add in the caster sugar, ground almonds, egg and almond essence and beat all these together. Then stir in the warm, melted chocolate. Spoon the mixture into the pastry case and spread out. Bake in the oven.

Serve warm or cold, with or without the blackberry sauce.

Blackberry Sauce

Wonderful colour and flavour.

Juice 2 oranges
1 heaped teaspoon cornflour
225g (8oz) blackberries (or raspberries) (frozen)
50g (2oz) caster sugar

Blend the orange juice into the cornflour and put into a saucepan with the black-berries and sugar. Bring to the boil, stirring all the time until thickened. Serve hot or cold.

Raspberry Crumble Tart

(Serves 5 - 6)

The raspberries are actually baked inside this delicious tart. The pastry is a cross between scone dough and shortbread. I use frozen raspberries for this recipe which means that it can be made all year round! It is equally good made with frozen blackberries. Be sure the fruit is completely thawed before use as this would interfere with cooking time.

Pastry:
150g (5oz) self-raising flour
150g (5oz) caster sugar
1 packet (100g) ground almonds
150g (5oz) butter or margarine
1 small egg, beaten
Quarter teaspoon almond essence

Filling:
225g (8oz) frozen raspberries, thawed
1 tablespoon sugar

Tin: Spring-clip tin 20.5 (8") diameter, greased. (5cm/ 2" is the maximum depth for the sides of the tin used - if too deep the top won't brown.)

Preheat Oven: 190°C, 375°F, Gas 5.

Cooking Time: 40 - 50 minutes, after 20 minutes reduce heat to 180°C, 350°F, Gas 4.

Mix together the flour, sugar and almonds. Add the butter, cut in lumps, and rub until like breadcrumbs. (This can be done very easily in a food processor, simply buzz together for a few seconds until like fine breadcrumbs. Make sure not to over buzz, or the mixture will turn into a dough.) Divide the mixture into 2 bowls. Put one aside (for the crumble topping). Add the beaten egg and almond essence to the other one and mix to a soft dough. Gather to a lump (it will be very soft) and place in the base of the tin and spread out with a knife, to cover the base.

Mix the raspberries with the sugar and arrange over the base, leaving a narrow margin all around the edge. Then using the crumbled mixture (that has been left to one side), scatter it in an even layer over the fruit and the base.

Bake in the centre of the oven, reducing heat after 20 minutes, until cooked (test with a skewer). It will have a light golden colour on top. Partially cool, serve warm or cold, accompanied with a little fresh cream or crème fraîche.

Chocolate Roulade

(Serves 5 - 6)

A special occasion dessert!

Roulades always strike me as highly amusing after all the whisking to fluff up the mixture, as soon as the sponge is removed from the oven, it promptly collapses! But that is the way it cooks.

200g (7oz) plain dark chocolate (good quality)
5 eggs (size 1) separated
150g (5oz) caster sugar
Half teaspoon vanilla essence

Filling:
100g (almost 4 oz) cream cheese
175ml (6fl.oz) cream
25g (1oz) caster sugar
Tablespoon fresh orange juice or Grand Marnier liqueur

To serve: Icing sugar

Tin: Rectangular tin (13" x 9"/33cm x 23cm), lined with baking parchment.

Preheat Oven: 190°C, 375°F, Gas 5.

Cooking Time: About 20 - 25 minutes.

Melt the chocolate. This can be done in a microwave on defrost setting (about 6 minutes).When melted stir well.

Put the egg yolks into a separate bowl with 75g (3oz) of the caster sugar and the vanilla essence and beat until creamy.

In yet another bowl whisk the egg whites until stiff adding in the remaining 50g (2oz) caster sugar.

Now mix the partially cooled chocolate mixture into the egg yolk mixture and beat together. Then add the egg whites in three lots, folding and stirring gently until thoroughly mixed through. Turn into the prepared tin.

Bake in the oven until the top is well risen and crisp. The sponge will be set but not very firm!

Take out and stand the tin on a wire tray to cool. Cover loosely with a piece of paper and a light cloth, to sort of keep in the steam and so soften the crisp top. It will collapse down as it cools !

Meanwhile whip the filling ingredients together.

Rinse out a tea-towel in hot water and lay out flat, with a piece of greaseproof paper (or baking parchment) as large as the sponge on top. Dust with icing sugar. Place a board (or base of a tray) over the sponge in the baking tin. Hold the board and tin together and invert them to turn out the cake. Lift off the baking tin and slide the sponge (top-downwards) off the board onto the prepared greaseproof paper. Peel off the lining paper. Trim the edge off the 2 long sides. Spread the filling over the top. Roll up gently but firmly (using the tea-towel to help pull it towards you) and don't be afraid if it cracks. Dust with icing sugar and serve.

Rich Chocolate Sauce

This 'deadly' sauce originates from Gundels restaurant, the most exclusive restaurant in Budapest. Delicious with ice cream, pears, profiteroles or any other way you like. The alcohol gives a wonderful bite to the flavour of the sauce.

15g (half oz) flour
25g (1oz) cocoa
200ml (7fl.oz) fresh milk
75ml (3fl.oz) fresh cream
75g (3oz) caster sugar
110g (4oz) dark chocolate (good quality)
Quarter teaspoon vanilla essence
50ml (2fl.oz) black rum or brandy

Put the flour into a bowl with the cocoa and stir in the milk to make a smooth paste. Then stir in the cream. Add in the sugar. Put into a saucepan. Bring to the boil, stirring to thicken. Add the chocolate (broken in pieces and heat slowly to melt it. Add the vanilla essence and the alcohol.

Serve hot or cold.

Rhubarb Meringue Pie

(Serves 5 - 6)

The combination of the crunchy biscuit base with the sharp flavour of the rhubarb, topped with the sweet meringue is really good.

Crusty Biscuit Base: (page 104)

Topping:
1 bunch rhubarb
Juice 1 orange
150g (5oz) caster sugar
2 eggs, separated
1 teaspoon cornflour

Tin: Spring clip tin 23cm (9") diameter.

Preheat Oven: Hot oven (200°C, 400°F, Gas 6).

Cooking Time: About 10 minutes.

Cook the Crusty Biscuit Base, leave in the tin.

Meanwhile, top, tail, wash, chop and stew the rhubarb in the orange juice (use no water). Sweeten to taste with 25g (1oz) of the sugar (remember the sugar in the meringue topping will give more sweetness).

Mix one (or both of) the egg yolks together with the cornflour (see note) and stir in a little of the partly cooled rhubarb. Add this mixture into the rest of the stewed rhubarb. Then cook over a gentle heat to thicken. Pour into the baked biscuit base. Whisk the two egg whites until stiff and then whisk in the remaining (110g/4oz)of the caster sugar. When really stiff, either pipe or spoon the meringue mixture over the top of the rhubarb filling. Bake in a hot oven until the meringue gets nicely golden. Remove the sides off the tin and serve hot or cold.

Note: One egg yolk is plenty, but if you have no other use for the second egg yolk include it also.

Fruity Meringue Nests

(Serves 6 - 8)

The contrast of the rich purple-red fruits is wonderful with the white meringue.

6 - 8 ready-made meringue nests
150g (5oz) blackberries (fresh or frozen)
150g (5oz) raspberries (fresh or frozen)
110g (4oz) strawberries (fresh only - if available)
Juice half orange
2 heaped teaspoons cornflour
50g (2oz) caster sugar

Partly thaw the fruit and put into a saucepan with the strawberries. Blend the cornflour and orange juice and add to the fruits in the saucepan. Cook gently until it boils and thickens. Sweeten with sugar. Cool and serve in nests at the last minute, accompany with whipped sweetened cream.

Fruity Fromage Frais

(Serves 4 - 5)

A tasty and speedy dessert. The combination of the slightly tart fromage frais, (low-fat very soft cream cheese, almost like a creamy yogurt), with the juicy fruits and the crunchy almonds is most attractive.

1 packet (100g) flaked almonds
1 carton (500g) fromage frais
About 25g (1oz) caster sugar
50g (2oz) black grapes
2 bananas, sliced
75g (3oz) strawberries, chopped
1 fresh peach or nectarine, chopped
1 passion fruit, scooped out (optional)
110g (4oz) raspberries, fresh or frozen (thawed)

To serve: Sponge finger (boudoir) biscuits (optional)

Brown the flaked almonds under a medium grill or in a moderately hot oven, being watchful not to burn them. Allow to cool. Put the fromage frais into a bowl and sweeten it lightly with the sugar. Halve the grapes and remove the pips, add to the fromage frais with the other prepared fruits. Stir in the toasted almonds keeping back a handful. Serve in individual glass dishes, with the remaining almonds scattered over the top.

Sangria

Just the drink for summertime, especially for a barbecue! *Because the wine is* well diluted it is not a very strong drink. If however you'd like *to change that -* add a generous "slurp" of brandy - but do warn your guests.

225g (8oz) sugar
275ml (half pt) water
1 eating apple, unpeeled
1 large orange
1 - 2 peaches (or use 1 small tin of peaches, drained)
A few strawberries
1 bottle of red wine (e.g. Spanish Rioja)
425ml (threequarters pint) of chilled soda water

First make a syrup using the sugar and the water - dissolving them in a saucepan over a gentle heat and then bring to the boil and boil for about 2 minutes. Then allow this to cool. All of this syrup may not be required because it is added to taste. Sugar syrup keeps for a number of weeks and so spare amounts can be kept, ready for use at a moments notice. Store extra syrup in a bottle.

Next, chop the eating apple (unpeeled) into smallish chunks (so they will fit into the drinking glasses) and do the same with the orange. The orange can be peeled or unpeeled as desired. I used to leave the skin on but now I prefer to remove it , making the fruit easier to eat. Also add the chopped peaches. If a few strawberries are to hand, they can also be chopped and included.

Pour the red wine into a jug or bowl. Add the fruit and enough of the syrup to sweeten to taste. It shouldn't be too sweet. Cover and chill until ready to serve and then just before serving pour in the chilled soda water (so that it is still nice and bubbly as you serve it). Sláinte!

Oranges in Lemon Juice   (4 - 5 Servings)

Simple but very tasty. Serve hot or cold.

6 oranges
Juice 1 lemon
Water (enough when added to lemon juice measures 275ml/ half pt)
50 - 75g (2 - 3oz) sugar (to taste)

Peel the oranges with a knife to remove all skin and pith. Then slice the oranges, across, in moderately thin slices. Dissolve sugar in lemon juice and water. Boil briskly for a couple of minutes. Add in the sliced oranges and heat thoroughly. Accompany with an orange yogurt or lightly whipped cream.

Cakes and Bread

Coffee and Walnut Cake

The cake is simplicity itself to make - just 'bung' everything into a bowl and mix! The inclusion of ground almonds and chopped walnuts gives the cake a nice texture. It is a one-layer cake. I usually bake it in my spring clip tin, normally used for cheesecakes. When cold, ice with Coffee Fudge Icing.

2 tablespoons instant coffee
2 tablespoons boiling water
175g (6oz) butter or margarine
175g (6oz) brown sugar (demerara)
3 large eggs (size 1)
Half teaspoon vanilla essence
175g (6oz) self raising flour
75g (3oz) chopped walnuts
25g (1oz) ground almonds

Tin: Spring-clip tin 23cm (9") diameter, greased.

Preheat the oven: 180°C, 350°F, gas 4.

Cooking Time: About 35-45 minutes.

The first thing to do is to dissolve the coffee in the boiling water. For the best flavour it needs to be very strong. Allow to cool.

Be sure butter (or margarine) is very soft. If stiff from the fridge, you can speed up the softening process by putting it, mixing bowl and all into the microwave for about 30 seconds. **Don't** let it melt. Into the softened margarine, put the sugar, eggs, vanilla essence, flour and the cooled coffee. Beat everything together well, but don't over-beat as this makes the mixture tough. (This is why it is so important to have the butter soft at the start.) Next add the chopped walnuts and ground almonds. Stir well. Put the mixture into prepared tin. Bake in the centre of the oven until cooked.

To check that the cake is cooked right through pierce with a skewer or knife, that should come out without any sticky particles adhering to it. Cool in the tin standing on a wire tray. Ice the top when cold.

Coffee Fudge Icing

This is very runny when it is made, but as it cools, it stiffens.

40g (1½ oz) margarine or butter
1 tablespoon instant coffee
1 tablespoon boiling water
175g (6oz) icing sugar, sifted to remove the lumps

Dissolve the coffee in the boiling water. Melt the margarine in a saucepan. Take off the heat and add in the dissolved coffee and icing sugar. Stir well. Leave for a little while, to cool until stiff enough to pour over the cake.

Cinnamon Meringues

A delicious combination of flavours. Small bite-size meringues, flavoured with cinnamon and filled with a mixture of melted chocolate and cream !

50g (2oz) icing sugar
50g (2oz) caster sugar
1 rounded teaspoon cinnamon
A few pinches of nutmeg
2 large egg whites

Tin: Flat baking tins line the base with baking parchment.

Preheat Oven: 100°C, 200°F, Gas half.

Cooking Time: About 2 hours.

Sift the icing sugar together with the caster sugar, cinnamon and nutmeg. In a separate spotlessly clean bowl, whisk the egg whites until just stiff and then start to add in the sugar mixture a little at a time whisking well between each addition. Use an icing bag with a "rose" pipe to pipe out small little meringues onto the prepared tins. In the absence of a bag and pipe, put mixture in small spoonfuls. Bake until the meringues are dried out. Cool on a wire tray. Before serving, sandwich the meringues together with the chocolate filling.

Chocolate Filling

Simple to make, this mixture takes some time to cool and stiffen.

150ml (5fl.oz) fresh cream
110g (4oz) dark chocolate, chopped (good quality)

Put the cream and chocolate into a small saucepan and heat gently until the chocolate melts. Mix thoroughly and bring just to the point of boiling. Turn into a bowl and allow to cool.

Chocolate Brownie Muffins

These are made using the all in one method, so the margarine must be soft. If it is hard from the fridge pop it in the microwave for a few seconds to soften - not to melt it .

200g (7oz) self raising flour
25g (1oz) cocoa
225g (8oz) margarine, soft
225g (8oz) caster or demerara sugar
4 large eggs
110g (4oz) raisins
50g (2oz) chopped walnuts or peanuts (raw)
1 eating apple, grated

Tin: Muffin tin or two standard bun tins. About 12 muffins or 20 - 24 standard sized buns. Use paper bun cases to line the tins.

Preheat Oven: 190°C, 375°F, Gas 5.

Cooking Time: About 30 - 45 minutes.

Sift the flour and cocoa together onto a piece of paper.

Put the margarine into a mixing bowl and beat it a little. Then add in the sugar, eggs and the flour and cocoa mixture. Mix everything together. Add in the raisins, nuts and grated apple and stir gently but thoroughly. Spoon into the tin filling generously so the muffins will rise up high when baked.

Bake until cooked and cool on a wire tray.

Brown and Oatmeal Bread Loaf

This recipe is an adaptation of my popular Brown Bread Loaf. The mixture is soft and easy to stir. The bread is baked in a loaf tin rather than in the traditional round shape. In fact, the mixture can be divided between two tins to make smaller loaves that cook more quickly.

225g (8oz) wholemeal flour
225g (8oz) self raising flour
175g (6oz) oatflakes (porridge-meal)
1 heaped teaspoon baking powder
1 rounded teaspoon bread soda
1 carton (125ml) hazelnut yogurt
1 large egg
Enough fresh milk to make 570ml (1 pt) liquid

To decorate:
Sesame seeds (optional)

Tin: One (or two) loaf tins 23cm x 12.5cm x 7.5cm (9" x 5" x 3" deep) well greased.

Preheat Oven: 190°C, 375°F, Gas 5.

Cooking Time: About 60 minutes. If mixture is divided in two, about 30 - 40 minutes. If necessary reduce heat to 180°C, 350°F, Gas 4, halfway through baking.

Put the first 5 ingredients into a bowl and mix together. Put the yogurt and egg into a measuring jug, whisk them together and then stir in the milk. Add the liquid to the dry ingredients to make a soft dough. Turn into the tin(s), spread out and scatter the top with sesame seeds. Bake in the upper part of the oven until golden brown and cooked through. Partly cool in the tin and then turn out to complete the cooling on a wire tray.

Making bread with yeast is quite a different matter to making bread with bread soda , the latter being the tradition in Ireland. You can prepare a soda bread and have it cooking in the oven, before you can say "Jack Robinson", whereas with yeast bread it will be at least 2 hours, if not more, before it is put into the oven. Admittedly, for most of that time, the prepared dough will be sitting quietly by itself in a warmish place, growing in size. The problem is if left too long, the dough will over expand and sort of collapse, so don't forget to put it in the oven! Once you get used to the rhythm of it, it is very easy.

Strong flour is the best to use when making yeast bread (strong flour is written on the flour bag). Strong flour is tougher and more elastic and so allows for the yeast to expand well, within the dough without it collapsing. A strong, electric mixer is a great advantage when making a yeast dough - as thorough mixing (kneading) is important - it is so much nicer to watch the machine do the hard work than to have to do it yourself! Because yeast works best in a warmish, moist atmosphere, the dough has to be allowed rise, almost to the size you want, before putting it into the oven. It will rise just a little more in the oven before the heat "sets" the bread.

Focaccia – Italian Savoury Bread

Focaccia, an Italian savoury bread, is baked on a pizza or sandwich tin, so it is flat and round. Before baking it is brushed with olive oil and scattered with coarse sea salt. Traditionally, it is served with drinks before a meal, but is also delicious with salads and soups.

To give a better flavour, I include some olive oil and chopped olives in the dough itself. It is delicious.

The following is enough for two breads. If you don't wish to cook two at one time, prepare all the mixture to "Step 3", and freeze the second one before baking.

25ml (1fl.oz) boiling water
200ml (7fl.oz) milk
1 sachet dried yeast
1 teaspoon sugar
120ml (just over 4fl.oz) olive oil
1 teaspoon fennel seeds , crushed (optional)
1 teaspoon herbes de Provence
15 olives, pitted (stones removed)
2 - 3 cloves garlic, crushed
450g (1 lb) strong flour
1 large egg
Salt and freshly ground black pepper
Generous pinches oregano

For the top:
3 - 4 ripe tomatoes, sliced
Olive oil
6 green or black olives, chopped
Coarse sea salt and freshly ground black pepper

Tin: 2 flat pizza tins or wide sandwich tins. Lightly oiled.

Preheat Oven: 200°C, 400°F, Gas 6.

Cooking Time: About 15 - 20 minutes

Step 1: Put the boiling water and milk into a jug with the dried yeast and sugar . Stir this lukewarm mixture and leave to stand while you prepare and measure out the rest of the ingredients. This allows the yeast to activate.

Put olive oil into a little saucepan with the fennel seeds and herbs. Infuse (barely heat) them very gently over a low heat for a few minutes, then strain off the seeds - this gives nice flavour to the oil , but it is optional. Roughly chop the olives and add to the oil with the garlic.

Step 2: Put the flour into a mixing bowl. Add in the milk and yeast, the olive oil and chopped olives and the egg. Season with salt, freshly ground black pepper and the oregano. Mix very well for at least 5 - 10 minutes. If the dough is stiff add a little more milk, as it should be fairly soft. If your mixer is not strong enough, use a wooden spoon to make the dough and then turn it out onto a board and knead it like the 'divil'. Don't mind if it is sticky at the start, as the dough toughens it becomes less sticky.

The dough must now be set aside to allow it to rise for the first time. Either put in into a plastic bag that has a little drop of oil rubbed around on the inside, or, be lazy like I am and leave the dough in the mixer, and wrap a **very** damp tea towel tightly over the bowl to prevent a skin forming on the dough. Leave until it doubles in size, then "knock it back" to its former size . This is done either by more kneading or simply turning on the mixer again - as I do! Mix or knead for a couple of minutes.

Step 3: Then divide the mixture into two and flatten into two rounds. Put onto the greased tins. (You can use a rolling pin but the surface doesn't have to be smooth). If preferred freeze one bread at this stage. Arrange the tomatoes on top, dribble a little oil over the lot and scatter with the olives coarse sea salt.

Cover each tin with a large upturned bowl (or place it into a large plastic bag, lightly oiled on the inside). Once again leave the dough to rise until nearly double its size. Bake in the upper part of the preheated oven until a nice golden brown and the bottom sounds hollow. Cool on a wire tray.

Variation: The tomatoes can be substituted with thin slices of aubergine, courgette or peppers.

If preferred, use all the dough to make one larger bread. Allow a few extra minutes cooking time.

The Romans were the first to record drinks made from fermented apples, but it was the Normans who brought the apple drink (cider) across the channel from the continent to these islands. Cider can successfully be used in cooking.

Fruity Cider Tea Cake

A delicious fruity cake. For speedy cooking, it is baked in a shallow rectangular baking tin and then cut in fingers or squares.

The fruit is steeped for a few hours in cider (much the same idea as a cold tea brack, when the fruit is steeped in tea). It takes about 50 - 60 minutes in a moderate oven.

225g (8oz) raisins
110g (4oz) dried ready soaked apricots, chopped finely, OR sultanas
1 carton (100g) glacé cherries, chopped
1 carton (100g) chopped mixed peel
275ml (half pt) cider
110g (4oz) caster sugar
Half teaspoon almond essence
350g (12oz) self raising flour
150g (5oz) margarine (or butter)
2 large eggs
50g (2oz) chopped almonds
40g (1½ oz) flaked almonds

Tin: Rectangular, shallow tin, 23cm x 33cm (9" x 13"). Line it with baking parchment (or greaseproof paper).

Preheat Oven: 180°C, 350°F, Gas 4.

Cooking Time: About 50 - 60 minutes.

Put the raisins, apricots, cherries and mixed peel into a bowl with the cider, sugar and almond essence. Cover and leave for 3 - 4 hours or overnight.

Put the flour into a bowl and rub the margarine through the flour until like breadcrumbs (I do this in my food processor, it only takes seconds, then I transfer the mixture to a mixing bowl).

Whisk the eggs lightly and stir into the fruit and cider mixture along with the chopped almonds. Pour the fruit mixture into the flour mixture and stir thoroughly. Pour the mixture into the prepared tin and spread out evenly. Scatter the flaked almonds over the top. Bake in the upper part of the oven until a lovely golden brown and the centre springs back when pressed with the finger. Stand the tin on a wire tray to cool. When cold lift the cake out of the tin and cut into fingers or squares as required.

Variation: Divide the mixture between two loaf tins and bake at the same temperature for approximately 1¼ hours.

Fruity Apple Juice Tea Cake

Made exactly the same way as Fruity Cider Tea Cake, but substitute the cider with apple juice.

Fruity Cider (or Apple Juice) Muffins

Make up either the Fruity Cider (or Apple Juice) tea cake mixture and put into a muffin tray and bake at same temperature - makes 18 muffins. These cook in about 35 - 45 minutes

Oatmeal Delights

The interesting twist in this recipe, is that the oatmeal is fried on the pan before adding it to the mixture which results in wonderfully light, crisp biscuits.

75g (3oz) margarine
175g (6oz) oatflakes (porridge-meal)
25g (1oz) flour
75g (3oz) caster sugar
2 large eggs
Half -1 teaspoon vanilla essence

Tin: Baking tin(s) lightly greased.

Preheat Oven: 180°C, 350°F, Gas 4.

Cooking Time: About 15 minutes.

Melt the margarine in a wide frying pan and add the oatflakes. Cook over a moderate heat stirring most of the time until the oatflakes begin to turn a light golden colour. Be careful not to let them burn. Remove from the heat and allow to cool. Stir the flour and 25g (1oz) of the caster sugar into the oatflakes.

Whisk together the eggs, vanilla essence and the remaining caster sugar until thick and creamy, then stir into the oatflakes mixture. Don't be surprised if the mixture seems to reduce in volume. Place in small heaps the size of a whole walnut on the prepared tins. Leave a little space between each, as the mixture spreads out a bit during baking. Bake until golden brown. Lift the biscuits (which will be soft) onto a wire tray to cool completely, during which time they will crisp nicely. Store in an airtight container.

Brenda's Fruit and Nut Ring Cake

Suitable for Christmas, this delicious cake is full of fruit and nuts and is a nice compact size. For best results choose good quality, nice plump dried fruit. Bake it in a ring tin as this makes for easy cutting. It can be eaten soon after baking or it can be stored for a few months.

Fruit and nuts:
225g (8oz) raisins
225g (8oz) sultanas
175g (6oz) dried, ready soaked apricots, finely chopped
175g (6oz) whole blanched almonds, chopped
OR 175g (6oz) walnuts, chopped
1 carton (100g) mixed peel
2 x 100g cartons glacé cherries, chopped
Grated rind half orange
1 - 2 tablespoons brandy or fresh orange juice

Cake mix:
150g (5oz) flour
1 teaspoon cinnamon
150g (5oz) butter
110g (4oz) brown sugar
3 eggs (size 2)
1 small teaspoon vanilla essence
1 - 2 tablespoons of fresh orange juice or brandy

To decorate: See end of recipe.

Tin: Ring tin 23cm(9") in diameter (see note at end of recipe). Line with baking parchment or greaseproof paper.

Preheat Oven: 170 - 180°C, 325 - 350° F, Gas 3 - 4. (If your oven is inclined to be hot, use the lower temperature.)

Cooking Time: About 1½ - 2 hours.

Put all the ingredients from the fruit and nut list into a bowl. Mix and leave to stand for about 2 hours or overnight.

Prepare the cake mix - first sift (or mix) together the flour and cinnamon. Using a separate bowl, beat together the butter and sugar. Then beat in the eggs, one at a time with the vanilla essence, adding a little of the flour and cinnamon mixture. Then stir in the remaining flour and cinnamon mixture. Mix in the orange juice and then stir in the fruit and nut mixture.

Turn into the prepared tin and smooth out.

Sit the tin in the centre of a large piece of tinfoil (shiny side facing tin). Pull the foil up the sides of the cake tin, to make tall protective walls. Tie in place with a piece of string. During baking, when the top gets brown enough, these tall foil walls can be pulled in together over the top of the tin, like a canopy to prevent over browning.

When baked, cool the cake in the tin standing on a wire tray.

To decorate: Brush top with apricot jam. Arrange alternative rows of **red and green cherries,** interspersed with rows of **walnut halves, whole almonds** and **thin slices of crystallised ginger.** Then brush with **apricot glaze** (made heating apricot jam with a little water until syrupy)

NOTE: Ring tin; If you find it hard to get a ring tin 23cm (9") in diameter you might like to do as I do and make your own. Use a round deep cake tin 23cm (9") in diameter. To make the ring hole in the centre, use an empty can of fruit (or beans! 400g/14oz size).

To keep the empty can in place; cut a circle of brown paper to fit exactly into the base of the deep cake tin. In the centre of this paper, draw the outline of the bottom of the empty can and cut out the hole very neatly, making a circle. (Repeat this process with baking parchment.)

The next step is to line the sides of the cake tin with baking parchment and like-wise line the outside of the empty can. (But first brush the surfaces of these with melted margarine or butter, as this helps the lining paper to cling snugly in place.)

To assemble; simply pull the prepared circle of brown paper, with the hole in it, right down over the can just as far as it will go (it will look a bit like a wide col-lar) - now sit the can with its 'collar' into the base of the deep cake tin. (Pull on the circle of baking parchment also.) It should fit neatly. Put a potato or a stone into the empty can to give it weight.

Mincemeat and Almond Shortbread

A real treat. Makes a lovely seasonal gift. A double layer of shortbread, with a luscious mincemeat filling in the centre. I find it more convenient to make each layer of shortbread separately.

Shortbread (enough for 1 layer, make twice):
110g (4oz) Butter or margarine
50g (2oz) caster sugar
Quarter teaspoon almond essence
110g (4oz) flour
50g (2oz) ground almonds or finely chopped almonds (see note)

Filling:
200g (7oz) mincemeat
1 tablespoon brandy or whiskey

Topping:
25 - 50g (1 - 2oz) chopped almonds

Note: To chop the chopped almonds more finely, buzz in a food processor.

Tin: Spring-clip tin, 23cm (9"), greased.

Preheat Oven: 150°C, 300°F, Gas 2.

Cooking Time: About 45 - 60 minutes.

Beat the butter until soft, then beat in the caster sugar and almond essence until soft and creamy. Mix together the flour and ground almonds and add to the butter/sugar mixture, mixing to form a crumbly dough. Use your hands to gather into a lump. (If the dough is a bit too soft - put it into the fridge to stiffen for about 15 minutes.)

Bottom layer: Roll out the dough, into small circle, place into the base of the tin and press (or roll) it out to fit into the tin. (Use a small container (e.g. mustard jar) as a mini rolling pin.)

Filling: Mix the brandy into the mincemeat and spread in a layer over the shortbread leaving a 2.5cm (1") margin all around the edge - moisten the margin with water.

Top layer: Roll out the prepared dough (on a floured round bread board) to almost the same size as the tin - then gently slide it off the board and on top of the mincemeat. Do this carefully, because once in place it is not easy to manoeuvre it around. Press the edges with a fork to seal. Scatter the chopped almonds over the top. Pierce the top layer with a fork, in a number of places to allow steam from the mincemeat to escape.

Bake in the oven until pale golden colour and cooked through. (If necessary lay a piece of greaseproof paper on top halfway through cooking to prevent the colour getting too deep.) When baked stand tin on a wire tray while cooling. Cut with a sharp knife when cold.

German Christmas Cookies (Makes about 18 - 20)

Spices, fruit and nuts are added to an egg mixture, which is placed in blobs onto rice paper and baked, giving lovely chewy cookies.

1 packet (100g) flaked almonds
1 carton (100g) chopped mixed peel
1 carton (100g) glacé cherries, chopped (optional)
Quarter level teaspoon <u>each</u> cinnamon, nutmeg and ground cloves
Seeds from 4 - 5 cardamom pods (optional)
Finely grated rind half lemon
110g (4oz) self raising flour
25g (1oz) ground almonds
2 large eggs
Half teaspoon <u>each</u> of vanilla essence and almond essence
110g (4oz) caster sugar

Rice paper

Tin: Baking tin(s). Place the rice paper in a single layer on the baking tins.

Preheat Oven: 180°C, 350°F, Gas 4.

Cooking Time: About 15 - 20 minutes.

Put the almonds, fruit, spices and lemon rind into a bowl and stir.

Mix the flour and ground almonds together in a separate bowl.

Into a third bowl, put the eggs, vanilla and almond essences and whisk until they are fluffy. Then add in the caster sugar and whisk until the mixture is really thick and creamy. Stir in the flour mixture gently and then stir in the fruit mixture. Place in spoonfuls onto the rice paper. Bake until a golden brown.

Cool on a wire tray and cut away the excess rice paper.

If liked the tops can be covered with melted chocolate or white glacé icing.

Rich Chocolate Cake

A lovely moist, one tier cake covered with apricot jam and a delicious chocolate icing. Melted chocolate is used in both the cake and the icing. I find the handiest way to melt chocolate is, to place the bowl with the chocolate, broken in pieces, into the microwave on the DEFROST setting for a number minutes. I learned not to use the HIGH setting, when I took a bowl in flames out of the microwave!

200g (7oz) plain (dark) chocolate (good quality)
110g (4oz) butter or margarine
110g (4oz) caster sugar
4 eggs (size 2) at room temperature
Half small teaspoon almond essence
4 rounded teaspoons flour
200g (7oz) ground almonds

Tin: Spring-clip tin 23cm (9") in diameter, lightly greased and line the base with baking parchment.

Preheat Oven: 180°C, 350°C, Gas 4.

Cooking Time: About 50 minutes.

Melt the chocolate and allow to cool a little. In a separate bowl, beat the butter until soft, then beat in the caster sugar. Then beat in the eggs one at a time, adding 1 rounded teaspoon of flour with each one (the mixture will curdle somewhat). Stir in the almond essence and the melted chocolate and the curdling will disappear. Then stir in the ground almonds. Put into the tin and spread out.

Bake in the oven until cooked. Partly cool in the tin on a wire tray, then remove the tin and cool completely.

To ice the cake: When cold, spread the top with **apricot jam** cover it with the **chocolate icing,** allowing some to dribble down the sides.

Chocolate Icing

This icing needs to stiffen in the fridge, so it can be made as soon as you put the cake in the oven.

150g (5oz) plain (dark) chocolate (good quality)
25g (1oz) butter
150ml (5fl.oz) fresh cream
50g (2 oz) icing sugar

Melt the chocolate, butter and cream together. Stir in the icing sugar and allow to cool (to thicken).

The Food Pyramid
A Guide to Healthy Eating Choices

A thumbnail guide to food choices for healthy eating are based on the food pyramid. The different food groups are on different shelves. The size of each shelf denotes the amount of that food that should be eaten in relation to the other food groups.

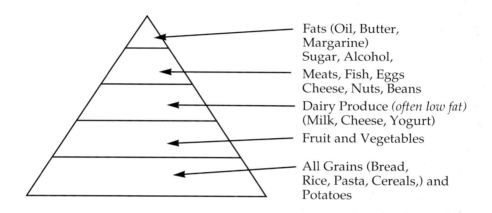

Fats (Oil, Butter, Margarine)
Sugar, Alcohol,

Meats, Fish, Eggs
Cheese, Nuts, Beans

Dairy Produce (*often low fat*)
(Milk, Cheese, Yogurt)

Fruit and Vegetables

All Grains (Bread, Rice, Pasta, Cereals,) and Potatoes

For example, the butter is on the tiny top shelf whilst bread is on the bottom big one.

Choose foods as near to natural as is possible or convenient and eat in moderation... but most of all enjoy it.

Recipes of previous book "Anything I Can Do..." Cookbook.

Recipes of previous book "For Goodness Sake" Cookbook.

Index of Easy Does It Cookbook